Fated Magic

The Wolf Pack
Book Two

by
Avery Gale

Dedication

I wish magic didn't have rules and wishes didn't have karma.

– Cathy Bryant –

CHAPTER ONE

LEANING BACK AND watching the sunlight dance over the water in the swimming pool, Kit looked down at her well-rounded belly and chuckled as tiny feet appeared and then disappeared beneath her taught skin as the twins nestled safely inside seemed to battle for position. "The sunshine looks like diamonds. Lord love a leper but I do love diamonds." When she looked over the top of her sunglasses at her friends, they were all staring at her as if she'd just grown another head. "What?"

It wasn't a surprise that her friend, Libby, was the first to speak. "Are you fucking kidding me? This is newsworthy information? Fuck me, you are annoying sometimes." Libby's giggle betrayed the fact that her words were spoken in jest. Libby Wells was a fully tenured professor of chemistry and neuroscience at NYU and Kit's best friend. The petite blonde with sparkling blue eyes and a wicked sense of humor was also the reason Kit had met Jameson and Trevlon Wolf last year. Libby and Kit's night of dancing had quickly led Kit to exactly what she had always tried to avoid…her mates.

"Agreed. Her husbands spoil her shamelessly and I'd be plotting her demise if she wasn't knocked up. I can't kill babies, that just wouldn't be right…killing a diamond slut is something else entirely. And calling her a witch is just plain anti-climactic since it's true." Julie Wolf-Edwards, one of the other women whose attention zeroed in on Kit. She was also cousin to Jameson and Trev and one of the most outspoken women Kit had ever met. She was a Harvard trained lawyer who handled all the pack's legal work and Kit had never seen the woman miss a single detail in anything she'd tackled. She was also a classic beauty with chestnut colored hair that she kept cut in a stylish bob and glorious hazel eyes that were always filled with mischief. Her cheekbones were perfect and she carried herself with an air of grace and elegance that reminded Kit of so many of the professional dancers she'd known.

Julie was married to Lance Edwards the enormously popular television actor and one of the few non-shifters living on the Wolf Pack's estate about two hours north of New York City. Kit knew that Lance did occasionally stay at their loft in So-Ho on nights when he was working late. But more than once, Kit had seen Lance coming in during the wee hours of the morning. Just recently she'd asked him why he'd driven so far at that time of night and he'd smiled conspiratorially. "Are you kidding? My wife is fucking *hot* and brilliant and my best friend. Why wouldn't I want to be in her bed?" Kit had fallen a little bit in love with him herself at that moment. She'd always liked him as an actor, he reminded her of Robert Redford in "Butch Cassidy and the Sundance Kid." And finding out what a genuinely nice man he was had only made her a bigger fan.

When the last of the crew hadn't weighed in, Kit turned to Angie Wolf-Michaels. "Well?" Kit inquired expectantly. "Aren't you going to add anything to the peanut gallery's litany of sarcasm?"

Angie tilted her head back, adjusted her enormous sunglasses, and flipped her blonde ponytail over her shoulder. "Nope, they've got this." Angie was a pediatric surgeon and researcher, she was also a cousin to Kit's husbands and the wife of Tristan and Nick Michaels. At five foot seven, she towered over the rest of them and her willowy frame and long blonde hair framed rich dark chocolate eyes. They teased her that she was going to meet herself at the door one of these days. Between her surgical patients and research, Kit didn't know how the woman functioned. This was one of the few times Kit had seen Angie sit for longer than it took to gulp down a meal. Tristan, the head of the pack's security detail, had been growling after Angie had been called away from dinner for the fourth straight night a few evenings ago that he was going to have to intervene before she wore herself completely out. After his comment, Kit had noticed that Angie did seem awfully tired and she'd certainly lost a lot of weight. And now Kit wondered if that wasn't part of the reason her friend had agreed to join them to enjoy some very rare, but much needed, down time.

They all giggled at Angie's blasé attitude and settled back to enjoy a few minutes where the only sounds were those made by the small waterfall at the other end of the pool and the breeze whispering through the nearby trees. Suddenly Kit felt like someone had thrown a bucket of ice water over her and steel bands were tightening around her chest. The feeling was oddly familiar and before she could even process everything her subconscious was already starting to panic. There didn't seem to be any logical explanation for the sudden change or the strange electrical charge that seemed to be buzzing all around her, but then her mind realized she was actually hearing words being spoken in the wind. When she heard it again she knew her subconscious had already registered the words whispering on the wind even when she hadn't noticed them the first time.

Soon… We'll meet again, soon. I'm coming for you, Kathleen. Joining me will make you a Princess of the Darkness and the pleasures of the world will be yours for the taking. Your children belong to me. Our combined power will be unstoppable. Don't fight this, Kathleen, this is your destiny. Are you willing to sacrifice your friends to deny me what is mine to take?

It was a hard won battle to break Damian's hold on her mind, but she finally snapped the mind link and sagged at the effort. *Why is he back so soon? Mother said it would take him years to regroup.* When she was able to refocus on her surroundings, Kit realized she was shaking like a leaf and was covered in a sheen of moisture that appeared to be sparkling. She looked up into the concerned faces of all three of her friends, but she couldn't shake the fear that kept pulling at her.

Kit was just superstitious enough to know it was a curse to even entertain the thought that things couldn't get any worse, because the Universe always seemed all too willing to prove her wrong whenever she'd made that mistake. But just as she was wondering how things had gone wrong so quickly her phone played "Witchy Woman" by The Eagles, the ringtone she'd assigned to her mother. The sound caused Kit to groan at how quickly the fates had responded to her momentary lapse. She was still debating whether or not to answer the call when both Jameson and Trevlon ran around the corner, their eyes wide with the terror felt by those who uncertain about the safety of someone they love.

Kit tried to not let her the soul deep fear of Damian's

threats and the icy hot spikes of fear his words had sent through her show in her expression, but she doubted she was doing a very good job of concealing the emotion since she was still trembling. Through the haze Kit could hear Angie talking to Jameson while Trev squatted down in front of her and ran the backs of his fingers down the side of her face. It was a gesture of pure affection and so typical of Trev. He was the charmer of her two husbands and she always appreciated the way he could center her with just a touch. Where Jameson demanded, Trev persuaded. His gentleness touched her soul...always.

"Baby, are you alright?" His words were soft and it was a perfectly reasonable question, and she cursed the damned pregnancy hormones when she felt the tears start to fall. He didn't even wait for her answer, he just scooped her up and headed into the house. Kit knew that she was awkward to carry now, but neither of her men ever uttered a complaint. She laid her head on his shoulder and hoped she'd be able to pull herself together before Jameson made his way upstairs.

"I'm sorry. I didn't mean to cry. I hate to cry. Crying makes me feel weak and out of control. And I do it all the dratted time. But you are just so sweet. And I love you so much. And it scared me, Trev. The voice. He's back. He said—" She didn't get to finish because Trev sat her on the cool counter in the master suite's bathroom and then pressed his lips to hers. Kit was sure that Trev had meant for the kiss to be short and sweet, but just as it always did, his kiss sent her from zero to fully aroused at the first sigh.

She could feel him reaching out and touching her mind with his own and she just let him in. One of the greatest gifts of being a mated wolf shifter was the ability to link to your mate's mind. The ability to feel the emotions of others and to speak telepathically had taken Kit a while to adjust to, because in the beginning it had felt as if she didn't have even the smallest bit of privacy. But once she'd learned how to shield herself from some of the intrusion, she'd quickly come to understand the real value of being able communicate without speaking.

Since she'd become pregnant immediately after being claimed she'd only gotten to shift into her wolf once. But that had been enough to convince her the experience was like none other. The exhilaration that that she'd felt running alongside her mates felt as they ran free under the full moon that night had been addictive and she had made sure their mind links were open each time they'd run since then so she had been able to enjoy it through them. Feeling the wind rush over their fur, the scents that filled the forest, and the joy of running all came through loud and clear and Kit couldn't wait until she could run with them again. *Come back to me, baby. I've gotten what I needed and I'm glad you enjoyed your little side trip.* Trev's voice whispered through her mind like a warm caress to her sensitized skin and she sighed with regret but pulled herself back to the moment.

"You sent that to me, didn't you? It was a distraction so you could find out what happened down by the pool, right?" She felt the tears start to fall again, but this time they were tears of love. Because he and Jameson were twins, they'd had a lifetime's head start on telepathy and even though there were times their abilities made her feel totally inadequate, she was certainly grateful for their skills today.

"You aren't inadequate in any way, baby. You just haven't learned everything yet. And heaven help us when you do." His boyish grin lit up his whole face and Kit was so drawn in that she hadn't even realized he stripped her out of her shorts and t-shirt. He leaned down and pressed a kiss to both sides of her pregnant belly and smiled as he ran his fingers over the tightly stretched skin. "They know I kissed them. They moved toward me. I've see them do it before. Watch."

Kit watched in absolute wonder as Trev moved from one her left side to her right, and the babies shifted and wiggled right along with him. "Oh my stars and streamers, they are following you like you're a magnet. That is absolutely amazing. Is this normal with shifters?" Kit was completely stunned and her heart almost melted at the self-satisfied grin on Trev's face.

"No clue, baby, but I can tell you this much, Damian isn't taking those babies anywhere. They belong to us…all three of us."

"And that is exactly where they will stay, kitten. Never worry that we won't move heaven and earth to protect you and our children. And that protection applies to your friends and family as well because if they are important to you, then they are important to us." Jameson was standing in the doorway with his arms crossed over his chest and his legs spread wide. He looked every bit the Alpha and pack leader that he was and he'd used a softly spoken tone of voice she had likened to velvet covered steel because if might sound seductive, but there was absolutely no allowance in it for argument.

Chapter Two

J AMESON AND TREV had been in a meeting in their office with the Tristan and Nick Micheals most of the afternoon. Tristan was the head of the Wolf Pack's security detail and his younger brother, Nick, was his second in command. Both were top of the line security experts and they'd been explaining some of the upgrades they'd recently completed around the estate's perimeter. The new equipment was going to offer state of the art protection for the entire pack, but the enhancements had been in response to the threats to Kit when she'd first become theirs.

Several months ago, Kit's grandmother had warned both he and Trev that the danger to Kit would increase as she neared her delivery date. No one had mentioned it to Kit because she had already been struggling with such extreme nausea her obstetrician had threatened to hospitalize her more than once and had advised her husbands to keep her exposure to stress at a minimum.

Jameson had never felt so helpless in his life as he had watching his lovely mate turn green and run from the dining room at some point during almost every meal for the larger part of five months. Even though all the damned books he'd read had said it would end sooner, the physician had assured them that exceptions were common and it would eventually pass. When Ruby had finally returned from a trip to the Congo and when she'd heard how ill her granddaughter had been, she'd shown up the next day with a small bottle of purple slime that immediately ended the problem. From that point on, Kit had been famished and everyone in the house had joyfully fed her anything and everything she'd asked for.

Ruby had returned each week with a new bottle and he'd cornered her the third week and asked what was going on. Ruby Stone was a force of nature and Jameson had a huge amount of respect for her and her magical abilities. Kit's mother was also a gifted witch, but she lacked Ruby's easy going attitude, and Carla Harris's continual criticism of her daughter hadn't set well with either he or his brother. Ruby had grinned and said she was only giving Kit vitamins at this point, but she was also teaching her a bit of magic and renewing the protections spells she'd placed on Kit and their children each time she visited.

They hadn't heard from Ruby in a couple of weeks and he'd asked Kit about it just last night while they'd been watching television. She had assured him it was perfectly normal. "Both my mother and grandmother fly off at a moment's notice when they are needed or the Supreme Council summons them. I just hope Granny Good Witch gets her happy self back here soon, I'm out of purple slime and when I tried to make it myself I had a problem in the kitchen."

Trev had burst out laughing. "A *problem*? Are you kidding? The cooks were terrified and banned you from the kitchen." Turning to Jameson he added, "Our sweet mate isn't allowed in there without supervision. It took the staff hours to clean the goo off every surface, including the ceiling." Jameson had looked at Kit in disbelief and just raised his brow in question.

"Well...yeah, they were pretty miffed. But banned is

really a pretty strong word. I'd really prefer to think of it as a recommendation. And I know you are wondering why you didn't know about this." Jameson had become amused as he'd watched her become suddenly interested in looking at everything in the room but him. "Well, I sort of bribed everyone so they wouldn't rat me out." When he frowned, she'd quickly added, "You know how you get. And I love you for being protective, I really do. But it can be a bit stifling at times and...well, I really do have to learn this stuff."

Jameson had fought the laughter threatening to bubble up, but he knew his lips had twitched and that she hadn't missed it when he saw her shoulders sag in relief. "Okay, kitten, new rules for you my lovely mate. We'll install anything you need for a learning lab in one of the back sheds, *but* you have to have your granny or mother with you and you have to wear a lead apron to protect the babies, and goggles...and gloves...and anything else I can dream up to protect you between now and then." She had reluctantly agreed and then he'd scooped her up and quickly made his way to their bed.

And now today, toward the end of their meeting, he and Trev had both been overwhelmed with an all-consuming fear that they had both known was coming from Kit. They'd both run from the room in a blind panic searching for their mate and had been quickly directed outside by one of their pack mates who was just coming in the backdoor. Jameson had been so overwhelmed with rage that he hadn't immediately registered her fear wasn't from someone that was actually present, but was from someone speaking in her mind. Whoever it had been was skilled enough to block both of her mates from hearing him. All they'd been able to hear was Kit's screaming fear and his soul had been set to boiling rage. *How dare anyone harm Kit?*

When they'd run around the corner of the hedge surrounding the pool area they had found Kit, pale as a sheet, covered in a cold sweat, and surrounded by her friends. When Jameson had seen for himself that she was unharmed, his knees had nearly buckled in relief. As soon as he'd touched her, he'd felt her fear race through him like polar ice. After pressing a quick kiss to her cool lips, he'd turned to Julie and listened as his cousin explained how Kit had suddenly started shaking and seemed to be staring off into space. Angie added that they had called Kit's name several times and she hadn't seemed to hear them and when they'd surrounded her, she hadn't even appeared to be aware anyone was near her. It hadn't been until Libby had given her a shake that Kit had finally seemed to return to the moment, but even then she'd been too dazed to respond to their questions.

In his peripheral vision he'd seen Trev tending to their mate while he talked to Julie, Angie, and Libby. Jameson hadn't been surprised to see his brother scoop her up and head into the house with her nestled safely in his arms. As soon as Tristan and Nick arrived, Jameson had headed to his office. He'd called Kit's father, but Richard Harris hadn't heard from his wife or mother-in-law since they'd left in the middle of the night a couple of weeks ago. Richard told him that he wasn't even sure where they'd gone, but he did know they'd both received calls from the head of the Supreme Council himself and according to Richard, that was highly unusual. Jameson quickly explained the threat that Kit has just received because the information had flowed freely from her mind to his with just a quick touch. Richard had promised to make some calls and be in touch. Jameson had given a quick update to Tristan then made his way upstairs. Listening to his brother and mate speak both out loud and through their mind link had calmed him and helped him refocus his energy away from his anger and directed it back where it needed to be...helping Kit.

He'd barely held back his laugh as he'd watched Trev distract Kit with his antics with the babies. They had both noticed the little tykes would shift toward them and been quite proud of it. Ruby had mentioned that both babies appeared to be magically gifted and the speculation was that it was even though she'd just conceived, her pregnancy had added to her power. And evidently that added power had helped Kit lock Damian behind the seal when he'd tried to harm her mates.

With Kit's due date approaching quickly, Jameson had been weighing the pros and cons of staying at the estate and having her deliver in their small clinic. A year ago they had spent an obscene amount of money building the small medical facility that even included a small, but state of the art operating room. Now that the threat had been renewed, he was leaning in that direction because it was easier to protect her here than it would be in a hospital. But he did understand his cousin Angie's concerns, as a physician she had pointed out some of the reasons a hospital with a well-equipped neo-natal unit might be a safer option. Jameson had planned to speak with Angie again before he broached the subject with Kit, but now he wasn't sure it could wait.

He and Trev both quickly stripped out of their clothes and moved their mate into the large shower. They kept their hands on Kit because she really did look like she had a very nice sized beach ball under her skin and he didn't doubt that her balance was being challenged more and more each day. Just before he had joined them in the shower, Jameson had taken the time to switch on the stereo so now the room was awash in the sweet piano music of Brian Crain. Kit was extremely sensual and Trev had noted that innate sensuality translated to her being very responsive to music. Jameson smiled to himself thinking about how grateful he was that Trev had noticed how music was able to calm her when she'd been so ill earlier in her pregnancy and they had immediately purchased everything the gifted pianist she favored had ever recorded.

Running his hands over her perfect ivory skin was like caressing wet silk and feeling her lean into his touch made him smile. "Does that feel good, kitten? You are practically purring, you know. And it is music to my soul to hear those contented sounds coming from my mate. Knowing that my touch ignites that fire in you is a serious turn on, love." He'd washed her long, dark red hair and conditioned it as well after he turned her back around and pulled her tightly against him so her back was nestled securely against his chest. He marveled at how perfectly she fit against him. Even though he and Trev were over a foot taller than their tiny mate, she still felt like she had been created for their arms alone.

When Jameson looked down over her soft shoulders he could see Trev was kneeling in front of Kit. Trev's voice was already rough with desire as he spoke to Kit. "Spread your legs for me, baby. That's a good girl. Now, just relax and let us make you feel better." As soon as Trev stopped speaking, Kit's head had fallen back against him and she'd immediately started shaking so Jameson knew Trev was working his own kind of magic with his tongue.

"Tell me what Trevlon is doing to you, my love." Jameson spoke against the outer rim of her ear and let his warm breath brush over the sensitive skin between her ear and hairline. The small shudder that moved through her like a wave let him know his effort had paid off.

Kit's breathing was becoming shallow and for several seconds Jameson wasn't sure she was going to respond because she seemed lost in a fog of desire. When she finally managed to speak the airy tone of her voice went straight to his cock. He would have sworn he couldn't get any harder, but he'd have been wrong. Speaking in a halting cadence, Kit's sweet voice floated on the steam surrounding them. "His tongue is magic and it's....Oh God. It's dancing in, over, and through the folds of my pussy and when he circles—" She hadn't gotten finish the narration before her scream of release echoed off the shower walls and she sagged limply in his arms. Her knees had folded out from under her, but he'd been ready and she'd barely dropped when he'd caught her in his arms.

The sparkles that always danced over her skin as she came were somewhat dimmed by the water in the shower, but they never failed to captivate him. The first time it had happened, both he and Trevlon had assumed they'd imagined it. Sex with Kit was always a soul-deep experience and each time they made love to her, it seemed as though they became even more tightly bound as a ménage unit. Jameson held her up until the trembles of her orgasm slowly abated. Looking over her shoulder, he saw her fingers tangled in Trev's hair. She was clutching him tightly against her belly and Trev was kissing their children through her tight skin. Jameson felt his heart skip a bit as he took in the beauty of the intimacy shared between the two people he loved most in the world. He tried to paint a picture in his mind because he never wanted to forget this moment.

Both he and Trev helped her dry her beautifully pinked skin and comb out the dark auburn hair that now brushed her lower back so the wet tips of the soft waves left water droplets along the top curve of her gorgeous ass cheeks. They dressed quickly and led Kit into their small living room. There were things the three of them needed to discuss and Jameson knew full well that if they gave in to the temptation and settled in their bed he wouldn't want to discuss anything except how deep he planned to sink his throbbing cock into her sweet channel. Hell, just thinking about it had pre-cum topping his erection and he groaned as he tried to find a comfortable way to sit in one of the wing-backed chairs. They'd settled Kit on the sofa and propped her feet up on the small mahogany table in front of her. "Kitten, I want you to know that we have already taken steps to increase security around the estate. Your granny mentioned a few weeks ago that the danger to you would increase as you got nearer to your due date so the security upgrades had actually started at that time."

Her eyes went wide, but to her credit she didn't complain about the fact she was only now being told about all of this. When he explained the questions and concerns that he and Trev had discussed with the security team about where their children should be delivered, he could hear the echoes of those same questions in her mind, and knew she had obviously been worrying about the problem too. He wanted to kick himself for not considering that as intelligent as their mate was, she would not have missed all the possible implications.

Glancing down, Jameson smiled when he saw her hand moving in slow, loving circles over her belly. Kit Wolf was going to be a spectacular mother, Jameson didn't doubt it for a second. He knew she was worried about being able to keep up with twins, but she still didn't fully understand all the benefits of pack life. And having an endless supply of willing helpers under the same roof was certainly going to ease the strain. But they'd also hired a couple of their younger pack members as nannies. The young women they'd chosen were the cream of the crop and had already been helping Kit as personal assistants, and she loved them both.

"Do you mind if I wait until I can speak with my doctor tomorrow and get his input before we make a decision? And I'd like to talk to Angie also since she'll be the babies' pediatrician. To be honest, both ideas have equal merit, and even though I'm worried about what might go wrong medically, I'm even more worried about the risk of them being kidnapped from the hospital." *Or who might get hurt in the crossfire when I defend them with everything in me if they are threatened. Because shattering a piece of bulletproof glass will pale in comparison.* Jameson knew she hadn't said the last thing out loud, but it didn't matter because it had roared through her mind like a cannon blast and he'd heard her loud and clear. And remembering how she had flung a ball of magic through the window of their bedroom to defend her mates made him smile. The glass in that room had been designed to withstand anything up to small missile fire, and with a simple wave of her hand Kit had disintegrated it and molecularly scattered Damian into the breeze. Jameson didn't doubt for a moment she could easily take down the entire hospital if her children were in danger.

TREVLON WOLF SAT in a chair just to Kit's right mirroring his twin's position on her left. He'd watched her closely as Jameson had explained the details of the new security systems and how they applied to her as she listened intently. But there was an odd tension in her muscles that he hadn't notice a few minutes ago. Trev wasn't entirely convinced it was all related to her safety concerns, and he'd also noted that the change seemed to peak and then fade. Kit had asked several questions but none had been particularly focused and that was unusual for her. When she and Jameson had finally stopped speaking, Trev leaned forward and clasped her small hand in his own. The pain she'd been masking from their mind link was impossible for her to keep concealed from his touch. Trev felt the hot lash of pain whip through his body and he was sure his eyes had widened immediately. "Kit? What's going on? Where is the pain? Don't try to hide this from us, baby. Out with it, *now!*"

Even though Jameson was the more recognized leader of their pack, the two of them were actually both pack Alphas. They were also both sexual Dominants and he'd deliberately used the Dom voice Kit always responded to so beautifully. He saw her eyes go glassy, "I'm sorry, I wasn't trying to hide the pain, but I didn't want you to worry. The doctor said I'd have these periodically because there is only so much room for these two little darlings to move and grow, and my body has to stretch a lot and that causes pain. But honestly, tonight it *is* unusually intense. I was trying to wait until we'd finished talking before calling Angie, but I'm not sure I'm going to be able to wait any longer."

Jameson was just hanging up his own phone and Trev knew his brother had already summoned Angie. While

Jameson took over with Kit, Trev dialed her obstetrician. He moved out of the room to speak with the doctor's message service because he didn't want Kit to hear the concern in his voice. But the pain he'd felt through her touch had been very intense and had certainly felt like more than muscles stretching to accommodate two growing babes. After leaving a message he called their pack's physician.

He moved back into the room just in time to let Angie breeze past him. As she moved into the room, Trev noticed the dark circles under her eyes and suddenly understood Tristan and Nick's recent remarks concerning their feisty mate not taking care of herself. He also wasn't surprised to see Nick following close on his wife's heels. No doubt the men were coming up quickly on the point where they would be intervening and just thinking about that caused Trev to grimace to himself. Angie had always been driven and absolutely brilliant, but she'd never been one to show the slightest hint of submissive behavior in public. Trevlon didn't doubt that the coming "discussion" was going to require both Tristan and Nick's very best negotiating skills. That thought had Trev grinning to himself because both men were extremely dominant and their "tact quotient" as Angie had referred to it was, in her words "shamefully lacking."

Trev greeted Nick with a nod as they both stepped into the living room. Nick Michaels might be ten months younger than his brother, but he was every bit as formidable. Nick was a weight lifter and it showed in his every move because his muscles rippled under the knit shirt that was stretched tight over his chest. His rugged looks often intimidated people until they got to know him, and then his killer sense of humor invariably made him the life of the party. As Angie carried her small black bag and moved over to sit beside Kit, Nick moved to Trev's side and asked, "Do you need me too get a car ready? We really do need to give some thought to putting several of the younger pack members through pilot training. If we had a helicopter we'd be able to get into the bigger hospitals a lot quicker."

"I agree and I think that is on the agenda and probably needs to happen sooner rather than later. Do you have anyone in mind?" Trev knew Jameson planned to bring this up at the next pack meeting, but he was interested in Nick's thoughts since he'd brought it up.

"Yeah, I think there are a couple of guys that would be excellent. And truthfully, I wouldn't mind learning as well." Nick's interest surprised Trev and he was sure it showed in his expression when Nick actually blushed. "I know, it surprised my brother and our wife, too. But the truth is, I was interested the first time we talked about it and I've even gotten the materials and have already been studying a bit."

Trev slapped his friend on the back and grinned. Just as he started to respond he heard a commotion coming from the other side of the room. Returning his attention to his mate, he heard her gasp and then watched as chaos became the name of the game.

JAMESON HAD LISTENED intently as Angie asked Kit question after question about the intensity, location, and frequency of the pain she was experiencing. Kit had answered each question even though it was with obvious effort and he didn't doubt for a minute she was greatly understating the pain. He'd repositioned Kit so her back was pressed into the corner of the sofa and her legs were over his lap so Angie could sit on the small table in front of her. When Angie leaned forward to remove the blood pressure cuff from Kit's arm, Jameson felt his sweet mate's entire body go rigid. And then, just as she cried out in pain, her water broke and Jameson suddenly found himself soaked.

He was completely stunned and blinked several times in surprise. It was Angie's laughter that brought his focus back to the moment. "Damn, girl, you don't do anything halfway, do you? Well this seals it—you're headed to the hospital, sister. Holy shit there was enough water in there to drown a duck. I'm surprised you weren't sloshing when you walked." He'd been looking blankly at Angie until he heard a small strangled whimper next to him. Turning to Kit, he saw tears streaking down her face and then her entire face seemed to crumble in sobs. *Fuck! What was wrong? Was she in that much pain?* Through his fog of confusion, he heard Angie's gentle words of apology, "Damn. Kit, I'm sorry. That was totally insensitive of me. See? This is why I should stay in the lab and operating room, less chance of me saying stupid shit and offending someone."

"It's alright. I know you were teasing, but I'm just scared because these babies aren't supposed to be coming just yet. I know the doctor said it was possible because they've gotten so big, but I'm really worried. And these stupid hormones are for the birds, I tell ya. These will be gone as soon as the babies are born, right?" Jameson had to give Angie credit for keeping at straight face at Kit's hopeful question when even *he* knew the answer.

"Well, it might not happen overnight. But you'll start feeling more like your regular self before you know it. Now, tell me what I need to pack for you. Or do you already have a bag ready?" Jameson chuckled as Angie turned into a virtual tornado of activity. First she'd made a series of phone calls and then she'd let Kit direct her to the bag in the closet that had already been meticulously packed. In the meantime, Trev quietly traded him places so he could discreetly move to another bathroom to clean up before they left. Jameson shook his head as he made his way out of the room, wondering to himself how the hell men involved in traditional marriages managed alone.

TREV HELPED KIT to her feet and got her in and out of the shower faster than he'd ever managed before. Touching her was sweet torture because he could feel each one of her contractions as well as the scorching fear racing through her mind. When it became clear the pains were too close together for them to possibly make it into the city, they moved quickly down to the small infirmary and clinic they'd built on the estate. Trev had heard Tristan making calls to get air transportation for the medical team and equipment Angie had already started coordinating. His attention was drawn back to the terrified woman in his arms as the next contraction started to build and Trev's knees nearly buckled at the intensity. He had no idea how women managed it and he suddenly had a lot more respect for those that were brave enough to go through it a second time. Seemed to him that once you knew how blinding the pain was, you'd avoid it like the plague in the future.

"Feel like you're in the eye of the storm, baby?" Trev smiled and stroked the side of Kit's face as they made their way down the bumpy path in a small cart. Even though she was cradled in his lap to cushion her from the majority of the rough ride, the discomfort was still clearly etched in the tense set of her jaw and the thin line of her pursed lips. Trev couldn't believe how helpless he felt and how deeply that affected him. The last two contractions she'd had were particularly strong and her skin had started to glow and sparkle with each tightening of her muscles.

After they'd settled her on one of in the beds at the clinic, Trev heard a commotion outside the door and sagged in relief as the medical team Angie had summoned strode into the room accompanied by their pack's physician. They unpacked their equipment with incredible efficiency, but he felt as if someone had tightened steel bands around his chest when he saw they'd brought intensive care equipment for the babies. He pulled the doctor to the side and asked why there were four of everything. The elderly man laughed, "Don't panic, Trevlon. I've been surprised more than once by a baby hiding behind his or her siblings, so I like to be ready. And sometimes equipment doesn't work like we want it to, so I've brought extra." With that, the elderly doctor moved to Kit's side. "Well, Kit, I see you have livened things up a bit. Did you forget that I was supposed to leave first thing in the morning for some fun and sun? So let's see what we can do about getting your sweet babies here all safe and sound, huh? My wife is going to be in a real snit if I don't take good care of you so I can relax while she spends me into the poor house on vacation."

Trev and Jameson both sighed at Kit's obvious affection for the elderly doctor they had known their entire lives. He and his wife were both members of their pack but didn't live at the estate. The minute the man sat down on the little stool between Kit's splayed legs, both he and his brother growled deep in their throats. Doc looked up and laughed. "Take it easy you two. Hell, I'm old enough to be her papa and you both know it. Now, places everybody, we have some very special babies to deliver."

Watching Doc switch from the affable joking fellow they all knew and loved to the all business professional as he examined their mate was unsettling because it was obvious the older man wasn't altogether pleased with whatever he'd discovered. Standing suddenly, Doc kicked the rolling stool he'd been sitting on behind him and started barking orders like the most jaded drill sergeant. The entire room exploded into a well-orchestrated symphony of precisely choreographed motion.

Chapter Three

A N HOUR LATER Trev stood at the side of Kit's bed and watched the new mama's eyelids finally drift closed. Her long lashes brushed over the dark circles under her eyes highlighting just how little rest she'd been getting the past few weeks. This pregnancy hadn't been a particularly easy one for his beautiful mate, but Kit had taken one look at their children and sworn to both he and Jameson that it had all been worth it. Holding his daughter in his arms while his twin held their son made every emotion, sound, hell even the colors around them seemed magnified somehow. Trev wasn't sure he'd ever know how to explain it, but now every worry he'd had about Kit and the babies was more intense than ever.

Letting his mind drift back to the conversation they'd had with Doc in the hall as his team had prepared Kit for childbirth, Trev shuddered. The terror he'd felt had been almost all consuming when Doc had explained that both babies were beginning to show serious signs of distress during each contraction and he was worried about their oxygen levels. Watching Doc deliver a boy and then a girl via C-section less than ten minutes later had brought tears to his eyes. Jameson looked up from watching baby Ryan sleep in his arms and smiled. They'd chosen that name because it meant "little king" and he would indeed one day become their pack's Alpha leader. Trev cradled Adana in his arms. The name meaning "her father's daughter" had been an immediate hit with them both. Catching Trev's eye, Jameson quietly spoke, "The money we spent on this clinic just paid us back a million times over. Doc told me outside we would have lost all three of them if we'd tried to drive into the city." Trev hadn't spoken with Doc because he'd stayed with Angie while she'd cleaned and examined both babies.

Jameson's words shocked him to his core and for the first time in his life, Trevlon Wolf thought he might actually faint. He was suddenly so overcome with fear for his small family he could barely keep his knees from shaking. He felt the blood drain from his face, and when he looked over at his brother Jameson merely nodded. "I know, I had the same feeling. Hell, I had to sit down out in the hall. The idea of losing Kit and the babies terrifies me. We have to figure—" That was all Jameson got out before Kit's mother swept into the room.

Trev nor Jameson were terribly fond of their mother-in-law. The woman was ice cold to her core in Jameson's opinion and the callous way Carla Harris had treated Kit when they had first met her left a very sour taste in both of their mouths. They tried to remember that her abrupt nature wasn't something they would ever be able to change so they made every attempt to simply accept her. Kit's father, Richard, on the other hand, was a wolf shifter with a gentle spirit and he obviously loved his daughter deeply. But their favorite member of Kit's family was definitely her spirited grandmother, Ruby Stone. Kit's nickname for the diminutive woman always made him smile. She had quickly become the adopted grandmother of the entire pack and everyone lovingly referred to her as Granny Good Witch. Ruby's colorful, straightforward personality and deep love for her granddaughter had endeared her to both Jameson and Trevlon immediately.

Kit's mother had fought alongside Jameson and Trevlon's parents as they'd fought to their deaths defending them when they'd been young adults. Ruby had whisked Carla away before Jameson and Trevlon had finally managed to unlock themselves from the sealed doors of the closet and stumble into the room finding all three of their parents dead. Until they'd met Kit, they had always believed the attack that had killed their mother and fathers had been directed at their mother. She'd been a witch married to two wolf shifters, just as Kit was now. In fact, their mating with Kit had been prophesized and it was that prophecy that had prompted the attack that had left them as their Alphas of their pack at such a tender age.

Of course, Carla being Carla was chattering a mile a minute when she hit the door and didn't stop even though they both cautioned her that Kit and the children were sleeping. If Trev hadn't been watching Ruby, he'd have missed the small flick of her wrist and he had to hold back his laugh as suddenly Carla's voice was little more than a hoarse whisper. Spinning on her heel with her hands fisted on her hips, she glared at her mother before straightening and waving her own hand in the air. Then speaking softly, she said, "Very funny, Mother. Now, if you don't mind, I'd like to see my grandchildren. Which one is which?" When she didn't get a response immediately, she waved her hand and Trev saw a swirl of glitter surround him for just a second before the white blanket around Adana turned a soft pink, and when he looked at Jameson, he saw his bundle of joy was now wrapped in baby blue.

KIT SIGHED AS she watched her mother's little display of power with amused resignation. *Honestly, the woman should have been an actress with her predilection for dramatic presentation. But even I can see the love in her eyes, those babies are what she has wanted for a very long time.* "Very dramatic, Mother. You could have given my husbands longer than a quarter of a second to respond you know. There wasn't any reason to…well, do what you did." Kit knew that her mother and grandmother both understood. As genetically linked witches they could easily read each other's magic. But all three men in the room were wolf shifters so they hadn't known that her mother had actually assessed both children and known in an instant not only the gender but that both Ryan and Adana held tremendous magical potential. They were both shifters as well, and as twins their magic would be magnified and enhanced by each other. Her granny had done the same assessment already weeks ago, and told Kit most of what her mother had just found out. She hadn't wanted to know the genders and Ruby had respected that. Now Kit had to hold back her gloating smile because it was obvious Granny Good Witch had cut her daughter out of the loop.

When Kit looked between Jameson and Trev her heart melted as their gorgeous smiles lit their expressions and reflected the happiness that she could practically see coming off them in waves. She knew that she would never tire of looking at her mates, and watching as they cradled the babies in their arms had been the sexiest thing she'd ever seen. Both men were six and a half feet tall and their broad shoulders a testament to their strength, so seeing them hold babies that had weighed in at just over six pounds was an incredible sight.

'Are you alright, baby?' Trev's voice sounded in Kit's mind and she blinked several times before she realized that she had been staring blankly at him. No doubt the residual effects of the drugs she'd been given were still clouding her mind. And even though she was still having trouble fully processing everything that had happened, she nodded. "Yes, I'm sorry I was staring. It just humbles me to see you and Jameson holding our children. And to see how peaceful they are in your arms. I'm going to remember this in the middle of the night too you know."

After maneuvering a huge vase of flowers onto the wide windowsill, Kit's dad stepped forward hugged her. "They are unquestionably the most perfect grandchildren in history, sweetheart." He kissed Kit on the forehead and then added conspiratorially, "And I'm awfully anxious to get my turn to hold them both, but that probably isn't going to come any too soon. One of the hazards of hanging out with two women who can zap you with lightning with just a flick of their wrist." He laughed and they watched as her mother and grandmother both commandeered a baby.

Kit giggled when her granny's clothes all turned pink as she held Adana. Even her usual red sequined high tops were now hot pink and sparkling like they were made of diamonds. When the elderly woman noticed her looking, she danced a quick jig as she moved toward the head of the bed. She turned to Richard and handed off the baby before grasping Kit's hand. "Kit, I'm sorry we weren't here. I heard what happened and even though we'd heard rumblings...none of us realized things had gone this far. You and I will talk more in a bit because you are about to have a whole lot of company." Ruby's eyes sparkled, and immediately the door burst open and Kit's room was literally filled with people in a matter of seconds.

CHAPTER FOUR

Four Months Later

D R. ANGIE MICHAELS leaned against the doorframe of the operating room she was leaving and grasped it with both hands, holding on to the metal frame as if it were a lifeline. She tried to catch her breath as the room suddenly seemed to be spinning around her and her eyes weren't cooperating either, having trouble trying to focus on her surroundings. She knew she had been on her feet far longer today than she was ordinarily, but it wasn't anything that she hadn't done hundreds of times before. She'd been struggling for several months to conceal her bone deep fatigue from her husbands because they'd been harping at her to cut back her schedule. Even though she knew they were right, she really was wearing herself into the ground, but they were being such asses about it that she just couldn't bring herself to give in to their Neanderthal demands. But this didn't feel like ordinary fatigue and she hoped she wasn't coming down with something.

Slowly moving to the side of the wide hall so she could steady herself with the rail, Angie made her way down the corridor toward the small waiting room. She needed to speak with the family of the young man she'd just operated on and being tired was no excuse to keep them waiting. He'd been injured in a very strange car accident that had killed both of his parents so Angie wasn't sure who she would find in the small surgical lounge. Rest was going to have to wait because she wasn't willing to let whoever it was wait any longer than necessary to hear that Braden was going to be fine. He was going to need physical therapy after his legs healed, but with some strength training, she was confident the fifteen year old would bounce back quickly.

Rounding the corner of the waiting room, Angie couldn't have been more surprised to see her friend Kit's mother sitting alone on the sofa casually flipping through a magazine. "Mrs. Harris?" She wasn't sure why she'd asked the question because Carla Harris was probably one of the most beautiful women Angie had ever met. Her face was one of those no one ever forgot or mistook for someone else so there wasn't any question about who she was. The woman was also insanely paranoid about having her picture taken and Angie smiled to herself because she knew the hospital's security staff was probably currently clambering to figure out what the hell had gone wrong with their surveillance equipment. Kit had told them about her mother's affinity for scrambling camera feeds and recordings anytime she was within their range and Angie couldn't wait to hear the "spin" the hospital administration came up with for the security lapse.

Carla stood and smiled as she extended her hand, "Hi, Angie. It's nice to see you again, although I wish it was under more pleasant circumstances." The minute their hands touched Carla's smile vanished and she quickly led Angie to a chair. "Spell me, dear, you are a mess. Sit down and let me help before we talk." Angie felt as if someone was pouring pure energy into her and then she relaxed and smiled inwardly as she realized that was exactly what was happening. She wasn't sure how long Carla sat with her before she suddenly felt better than she had in weeks. *I have no clue what she did, but she is my new best friend. I wonder if Kit can do this?* Angie was startled when Carla laughed out loud and Angie realized that she'd never seen Kit's mother be anything but cool and distant. Even when she'd been holding her grandchildren, who she clearly adored, she seemed almost detached. "Oh dear, you really might as well say all of that aloud, you know, because I can hear it all. And yes, I'm well aware that I come across as a heart-less bitch, but I assure you there is a very real heart beating in my chest. And the young man that you just worked so tirelessly to help owns a big piece of it."

Now that she felt more herself, Angie looked at the woman sitting next to her with an entirely new level of respect. "Okay, talk to me. You know I can't talk with you about my patient unless I know you are his next of kin or guardian."

Carla merely nodded, "I understand and I wish more than I can say that I could tell you that. But we both know that isn't true and I won't lie to you. What I can tell you is that he is in a lot of danger. Did you notice that every person who has dealt with him was exhausted? And the fact that you are so drained is something my mother and I are going to explore, I assure you. Do you have any family in Ireland by chance?" Before Angie had even been able to answer her question, Carla went on. "His magic is drawing healing energy from each of you every time you touched him, so naturally you got the worst of it as his doctor, but still." Angie watched as Carla seemed to consider her words carefully before continuing. "The accident that took his parents was a carefully staged attempt to kidnap Braden."

Even though Carla's words had shocked her, Angie moved as she planned to head back down the hall and check on the young man who looked more like a boy than a man. His crystal blue eyes and curly blonde hair had captured Angie's heart and she'd felt oddly drawn to him. Carla stood as well and reached for Angie's hand. "He's safe. At least for a while. I won't be able to conceal him for very long though and then I'm going to have to find a place that is safe for him to recover. And eventually he'll need to be placed with a magical family if I can find one that isn't afraid to take him." Carla's eyes were shining with unshed tears and she seemed lost in thought for a few minutes. She finally continued explaining that the man and woman Braden had been riding with weren't really his parents, but a foster family who had been trying to protect him. Angie listened as Kit's mom explained that his mother had died during childbirth. The little boy had lived with his shifter father in both Ireland and Scotland until his magical abilities had become too hard to disguise any longer. They'd moved numerous times but even with the Supreme Council's help, it had been impossible to stay ahead of the dark forces that wanted the child.

"This isn't the time to explain all the particulars of his birth, but suffice to say there is a very real connection between that sweet boy and the forces that are pursuing Kit and her children."

"What do you mean?" Angie had never understood all of the intricacies the magical community even though she knew there were some mystics in the more distant branches of her own family tree. She'd been raised to embrace her shifter heritage and had often wondered about her father's family who had come over from the same countries that Carla had just mentioned. Just thinking about being forced to hide who she really was from the world made Angie almost shudder with disgust. She couldn't imagine how difficult it must have been for the young man currently swimming his way back to the surface of consciousness.

Since Braden's father had been a shifter from a Celtic area where Angie had extended family, she'd listened patiently as Carla described the battle that had claimed the life of Braden's devoted dad. As Carla had spoken, every hair on the back of Angie's neck stood straight up. She had never believed in coincidences and she vowed to herself to ask Julie to look into Braden's family history. As the Wolf Pack's attorney, Julie had the means to get information much quicker than Angie would.

"That is where my mother and I were during the last weeks of Kit's pregnancy. We had been shuffling Braden from family to family trying to find one that was willing to take him, but most were just too frightened. It isn't him you understand, because he is a charming youngster. But everyone is afraid of the consequences of housing and protecting him. If I hadn't been downtown today and felt the magical shift, they would have gotten him."

Angie mind was whirling at the information Carla shared. "Does Kit know about this? Have you mentioned it Jameson and Trevlon?" She couldn't imagine their pack not protecting a child and she wondered if Carla had considered it. For the first time since meeting her, Angie saw vulnerability in Carla Harris's eyes. And it was in that moment Angie got a glimpse of a protective mother buried deep inside Carla Harris. She was worried about exposing her daughter and grandchildren to danger and Angie felt her opinion of Carla reverse itself. Grasping Carla's hand in her own, Angie asked, "Do you mind if I talk to my pack about Braden?"

AFTER A SERIES of calls, Carla had arranged for Braden's continued protection at the hospital then Carla and Angie headed to the Wolf's country estate. The car had barely stopped when Angie's door was pulled open and Nick pulled her into his arms. He didn't say anything. He just pressed her tightly against his chest. Despite the fact they were mated, Angie knew that both Nick and Tristan regularly locked her out of their mind link because they worried about adding to her burdens by letting her hear their problems. Angie had tried to explain that not knowing and feeling excluded was actually more exhausting, but she never seemed to be able to convince them. After several moments, she finally felt his shields begin to ease. '*I was so worried about you. You were being drained and there wasn't anything we could do.*'

Angie pulled back and looked at him completely shocked at what he'd just revealed. "How did you know? Who told you?" Her words had come out sharper than she'd intended, but she didn't bother trying to retract them.

Nick cocked his head to the side and raised his brow at her in question, probably more at her tone than the actual meaning of her questions. But it was Tristan who answered from behind her. "Love, do you really think we aren't checking on you all day—every day? Do you honestly believe that we reluctantly let you leave here in a stupor every morning and then we don't watch over you?" His words couldn't have surprised her any more. It had never entered her mind that they were watching over her. Her heart suddenly felt like it would burst with love for the two men she'd married and then had obviously shamefully neglected.

Tears streamed down her cheeks and she stepped forward into his arms and pressed her cheek against Tristan's chest, letting his warmth comfort her. When she finally pulled back he tilted her chin up and smiled. "We have some things to talk about after this meeting. But for now, come along, let's see if we can't help a young man that I believe has captured your heart." That had been all it took to push her fragile emotions over the edge and she felt like she was in a free fall into an emotional abyss. Nick picked her up and they made their way up the wide steps. When they walked through the front door, Carla reached for her hand and her touch stilled the roar of emotions swirling in Angie.

"You're going to be fine, Angie. You've pushed yourself much too far and then the drain on you today was nearly your undoing. I'm sorry things went so far, but I couldn't get to you. Those nurses that guard the operating rooms missed their calling, they'd make damn fine prison guards. One of them actually called me a witch and thought it was an insult, the twit. She probably won't be at work for a few days by the way, I'm fairly certain she isn't feeling all that well." The glint in Carla's eye was pure Mistress of Mayhem and Angie laughed despite herself. "There, that is much better. Now, let's get into this meeting before my son-in-laws add another black mark to my already heavily scarred card."

When the sophisticated woman turned on her heel and walked down the hallway with the grace and elegance of royalty, both Nick and Tristan blinked as if they'd just seen the woman for the first time. Nick turned and looked at Angie and whispered, "Who was that and what has she done with the ice cold bitch that we all know as Kit's mother."

Laughter sounded from down the hall, "I heard that you know."

CHAPTER FIVE

KIT PACED THE length of her husbands' office like a caged animal during the entire meeting regarding the boy her mother simply referred to as Braden. Jameson hadn't hesitated a moment in his agreement to take the teenager in and the rest of the meeting had been taken up with logistics and planning for his safety as well as the safety of everyone else living at the estate. Kit was in favor of taking him in and knew her friend well enough to know where he'd be staying once he arrived. It was obvious that Angie had felt a very real connection to the young man and Kit was relieved that everyone was rallying around him. Her restlessness had nothing to do with Braden...no her frustration was directed entirely at her two Alpha mates.

Try to tell me that I have to wait for the next full moon to run. Damn wolves think they can rule the world just because they are the Alphas of the pack. Don't think so, fellas, I am running tonight if I have to leap out of a damned window naked and fly into the forest on a damned broom. She'd always detested the image of witches on brooms because it was about the most ridiculous bit of imagination in history if you asked Kit. Brooms? Really? Like any self-respecting witch needed a damned broom.

Spending the past four months cooped up in the estate was taking a toll on her sanity and if she didn't get out soon she was going to be loon. At first she'd been too busy with the babies to worry about the fact she often spent the entire day in her pajamas. But the only thing that had kept a lid on her growing frustration was the fact she'd been spending a lot of quality time in the gym expending copious amounts of energy in every sort of physical outlet she could find. Well, all but the one she wanted to be enjoying. Her husbands had, for some reason, decided vanilla sex was more acceptable for a "mother" and she was seriously considering drowning them both.

How can anyone who can be replaced by a battery operated device consider himself the Lord and Master of his Kingdom? I didn't even get a honeymoon. Nope I went straight from caught to mated to knocked up. Once they got what they wanted all was well in the Wolf brothers little Alpha paradise. Whoever decided men should be the leaders of a pack or any other group really needed to study ancient history. Fat fairies will fly over Philly before I settle for vanilla sex for the rest of my life. It's just mean. Show me all the fun of kink and then take it away? I don't fucking think so.

She'd finally gotten the go-ahead from the doctors to shift and run tonight and then Jameson had "suggested" that she wait until the next full moon because of the meeting she was currently ignoring. Well she'd be showing them a thing or two in a couple of hours because she had already made arrangements for the twins to spend the night with a couple of their nannies and she planned to make an appearance in the forest come hell or spell.

🐾 🐾 🐾

Trevlon watched Kit pace and thanked every great spirit he'd ever heard praised that he wasn't in charge of the meeting he was currently sitting in because there was no way he would have been able to keep a straight face. He was struggling as it was and the attention wasn't directed at him. Kit's restless energy was palpable and even her mother had tried unsuccessfully to calm her. Actually, Trev didn't even think Carla's words had penetrated the internal hissy playing out in Kit's mind.

Oh, their pretty little mate might think she was shielding her thoughts from both he and Jameson, but she was still too new to that game to actually carry it off when she was obviously so lost in the moment. Trev had struggled several times to keep from laughing out loud and now that she'd basically told them how much she missed their Dominance, they would be reminding her just how good they were at gaining her submission. But he was disturbed that she'd obviously felt slighted by the honeymoon issue. It was a detail they had indeed let slide and something that needed to be rectified—soon.

Trev had been so busy considering ways to bring their beautiful little witch to heel that he'd almost missed one very crucial thought that she'd spoken a little too clearly in her mind. Trev knew that Jameson had been trying to ignore most of her ravings so he could finalize the plans for Braden's protection. But even as distracted as he was, Trev felt the shift in Jameson and knew his twin hadn't missed the last nail Kit had just pounded into the coffin that her upper hand was being buried in.

When she'd admitted that she had actually faked her orgasm that very morning while Jameson had made love to her, Trev had nearly swallowed his tongue and Jameson had literally come up out of his enormous leather chair and growled, "Out! Everyone out right now. Tristan, you finalize this. Take it anywhere, but I want everyone out of this room *now*."

Kit had frozen in her tracks and for the moment her mind had gone completely silent as she struggled to comprehend the implications of what had happened. Trev couldn't hold back his smile when she tried to scamper out of the room with the others who were scattering like fall leaves in the wind. Just as she reached for the doorknob, Jameson's deep voice rumbled through the room and Trev knew he'd spoken through clenched teeth. "Don't even try it, kitten."

KIT'S MIND WAS racing as she tried to remember what she had been thinking about when she had felt the energy in the room shift as if a storm had suddenly moved in just before Jameson suddenly kicked everyone out. *And he turned red, don't forget that because no doubt that is a pretty important clue, Kit. Oh crap on a canary I am in deep shit and I can't even remember why. How can I construct a defense when I don't remember….oh shit!*

"Oh shit, indeed, mate." When she slowly turned to face Jameson he had moved very close and she hadn't even realized that she was now easily within his reach. Just as she let her mind consider fleeing, he reached out and wrapped his huge mitts around her upper arm. "Really, kitten? You think you can run"

"Well, it probably would be prudent to give you a little breathing room because you do seem a bit miffed. And since I am evidently at the eye of the storm and I just can't for the life of me imagine why…" She even tucked her chin and batted her eyes innocently for effect, hell, Scarlet had nothing on her. But it was a wasted effort because his hold just got tighter as he led her to the center of the room.

"Well even though it might actually be in your best interest if I expended some of the energy that is suddenly boiling inside me, it isn't going to happen—yet. We'll play the chase game later. We have a few things to *discuss* and most of that is going to take place elsewhere as well. But first...do you trust me?" When she nodded he added, "Do you trust Trev?" Again she nodded. This time he held out his hand and in her peripheral vision she saw Trev lay something black in Jameson's open palm. "Turn around, kitten."

With no small measure of reluctance, fear and anticipation all swirling in a bubbling cauldron of emotion, Kit slowly turned. Every instinct in her screamed that you never turn you back on an enemy, but despite the fact she knew he was angry with her, Kit also knew they loved her and would never truly hurt her. "Good girl, close your eyes, kitten." When she let her eyelids fall, she immediately felt the cool silk slide into place as Jameson quickly secured the blindfold into place.

Kit knew her breathing was already becoming quicker as the excitement began to take root. God but she'd missed this rush. And even though she knew he was angry and would no doubt make her pay in spades for faking her release, Kit also felt completely safe in their care. Her exhilaration at having "her men" back was tempered very little by her fear of the unknown and quite frankly, if they never fucked her in that damned missionary position it would suit her just fine.

CHAPTER SIX

J AMESON HAD LITERALLY seen red when he'd heard his mate's confession during her mental tirade. When her frustration had started he'd managed to tune most of it out because he'd known Trevlon was listening in. But her admission that she had faked a climax had stunned him beyond anything she'd ever said or done. Hell, he was almost as mad at himself for having missed it as he was at her for thinking it was acceptable. Every single cell in his body had changed from pack Alpha to Dom in the blink of an eye. Hell, no self-respecting man appreciated that sort of disrespect, and to an Alpha who was also a sexual Dominant, it was a blatant throw-down challenge. There was no way he would let this go unpunished. And Jameson had every intention of showing his precious mate just how many ways he could indeed punish her. He'd seen Doms in clubs punish their subs in very creative ways for much less.

Wrapping his large hand around her much smaller one, he felt the slight tremble she quickly brought under control. He leaned close and let his words drift over her ear in a move carefully calculated to both arouse and alarm. "We'll see if you feel the need to fake your release after my brother and I finish with your punishment, sweet mate. And I assure you we can punish you in ways you have yet to even imagine." Reaching around her, he gave her ass a solid whack. "This ass is ours and you racked up a whole lot of punishment in a very short amount of time, kitten. You'll do well to remember your manners as we take care of this too, kitten, because we'll just continue until we believe you have learned the lesson well enough. Now come along."

He let Trev take the lead so all the doors he directed her through were already opened keeping her disoriented. They deliberately led her in circles and up and down various sets of stairs so she'd be totally confused about where they'd led her. They'd never taken her into their play room and they didn't really want her to know its exact location just yet. Blocking her from their mind link, Jameson spoke directly to his brother. *'Take the lead, I don't want her to hear the beeps of the keypad.'* Turning his back to Trev to shield some of the noise, Jameson cupped his large hand over both her ears in a move that was both purposeful and possessive as he crushed his lips against hers. Kit's response was equally explosive and Jameson knew in that instance that their sweet woman had indeed missed this aspect of their mating.

Kit had responded well to being dominated from the beginning, but after they had been formally mated she had become particularly responsive. Obviously he and Trev had underestimated her need for their dominance, and that was something they would be rectifying in short order. But right at this moment, feeling her molten reaction to his kiss caused him to growl deep in his chest and he fought back his body's demand to shift. Focusing on the soft mewing sounds coming from his mate was causing him to lose his concentration and he needed to refocus from sinking into his own need to how he could most effectively dominate her. Her breasts were larger now that she'd had given birth to their children and feeling their softness pressing against his chest sent a spear of primal need straight to his cock.

When he finally pulled back from the kiss they were both panting and the smell of Kit's arousal was surrounding them like a cloud of temptation. As soon as he moved her into the play room he felt her stiffen. *Aha she feels the difference in the energy of this room and even though she can't see where she is, she knows it isn't a place she has been before.* He was counting on that unfamiliarity to feed her desire as well as up the stakes of the punishment, because he really was completely pissed off about the fact she'd hidden her needs from them. That, as well as faking an orgasm, were pretty significant offenses and he planned to make it a lesson she didn't forget for a good while.

Jameson stepped back out of her reach and then silently circled around so he and Trev switched sides. Trev's amused voice floated into his mind. *'It won't work, you know. She can tell us apart by energy alone.'*

'I just want to keep her guessing. She is too smart for her own good and a bit of discomfort and scrambling will be good for her. I'm pissed that she faked the orgasm, but I am fucking outraged that she felt the need to. How did we let this get so out of control?'

'No clue, brother, but we have obviously been neglecting out little witchy mate. That needs to stop now.'

Jameson couldn't have agreed more and he let every bit of his Alpha command in voice lace through his one word command, "Strip."

🐾 🐾 🐾

KIT HAD BEEN nervous as they'd led her through various hallways and passages, but not for the reasons her husbands had assumed. She had known where they were leading her and even if she hadn't already known where their play room was, she would have been able to track their attempts to confuse her. The fact that they both continually underestimated her magical abilities usually worked in her favor so she had been leaving them to enjoy that delusion. But really...their lame ass attempt to switch sides and confuse her was just plain insulting. The real reason she'd been nervous was because she'd been worried they would suddenly change their minds and she'd be stuck with vanilla sex until the next millennium.

Even though it was true of all D/s relationships that the Dominant only has power that the submissive *allows* him or her to have, it was particularly true in their case. Kit knew that her magical skills, even as new and underdeveloped as they were, already exceeded their ability to control her physically if she didn't allow it. But she also knew their real power over her wasn't physical, but it was the ropes of love they'd wrapped around her heart that were where their real power lay. Their recent "kid-glove" treatment had hurt her. They were not only denying her the kink that it took to drive her body to the heights of pleasure it had become addicted to, but they had basically locked her away from who they really were, and that exclusion had been the worst blow they could have delivered.

At Jameson's command, she slowly began removing her clothing. A part of her wanted to bask in the warm glow of the moment while another part was secretly hoping to rack up a few more punishment points. If they wanted her to *behave*, Kit seriously doubted this was going to be the way to meet that goal because quite frankly, they made punishment feel awfully good.

Their playroom smelled of fine leather and the lemon oil that was used to buff the wooden equipment to a brilliant sheen. Kit had discovered this room quite by accident one day not long after she and the Wolf brothers had become mated. She remembered that she'd just laid her hand on the key pad and the door had opened so she'd quickly stepped through. The entire room was made to look exactly how her imagination had always pictured a Middle Age's dungeon. Because they were actually two full levels below the main floor of the estate's large main house, the floor and outer walls were rock.

Even blindfolded, Kit knew exactly where she stood in the room and the shivers of excitement that pebbled her nipples and sent goose bumps over her bare skin were pure anticipation. She had lain awake so many nights after she'd first found this room and wondered why they hadn't brought her here to play. At first she'd wondered if they'd assumed it was because their relationship was so new, but as time had worn on and she'd ballooned to the size of small beached whale, she had feared it was because they just didn't want to look at her that closely. After the twins arrived, she'd slimmed down quickly thanks to nursing two very hungry babies for three months before it had become just too difficult to manage. *Those kids definitely have shifter appetites and this mama just wasn't able to keep up.* But even regaining her figure quickly hadn't brought her here and she'd begun to wonder if it was reserved for "others". And just the thought of her mates dominating another submissive had turned her stomach.

She waited for Jameson's next command, and the stillness of the room was unnerving. The stone walls should amplify each and every sound, no matter how cleverly disguised, so the fact it was deathly quiet could only mean one thing...she'd let her mind's shields slip enough that they were listening to each and every thought swirling around her mind with the force of a hurricane...and she was digging herself in deeper by the moment.

TREVLON WOLF WAS, according to most people, the more affable of the two of them. Jameson was the Wolf brother most prone to simply demanding the compliance of others. Trev understood that Jameson usually dealt with things in that manner more as a matter of expedience than in an effort to exercise his power, but it was still the way he was seen by others. Trev, on the other hand, was seen as the charmer. He and Jameson had learned early on that playing the opposite sides of the stage usually offered them the best chance of reaching the entire audience. It was a complete fallacy that he was the "more lenient" of the two of them as Kit was about to discover.

He'd been listening to her rant upstairs as she had paced restlessly during the meeting and understood immediately what the problem was and precisely how they could rectify it. But he hadn't known until just now how long it had actually been an issue, and that information didn't sit well with him at all. Trev agreed with Jameson that she shared the blame by not addressing it with them, but Trev also understood there were several factors at play. First, their relationship was so new that they hadn't been able to build the level of trust that sort of soul baring probably required, and then she'd been so ill for several months that treating her as if she was fragile had become more habit than was necessary. But ultimately, the blame rested squarely on their shoulders because as the pack Alphas and as sexual Dominants they were more than adequately trained to read the needs of the people around them. And the realization that they'd misread the person who was usually standing right between them was uncomfortable and humbling.

Stepping forward, Trev tunneled his fingers in her long, wavy red tresses and pushed her hair over her shoulders as he brushed his lips against hers. "I'm going to braid your hair so it doesn't get caught in anything while we are in here, baby." He'd already put a thin strip of leather in his pocket as he'd pulled various toys out of the armoire when he'd first entered the playroom. Walking around behind her, he sectioned her hair and began weaving it together as Jameson tossed his shirt aside and toed off his boots and socks. They both preferred being barefoot in this room so their footsteps were silenced. Not knowing exactly where a touch might come from added to a submissives mind set and also gave their Dom the added advantage of surprise, and with their mate, they needed every edge they could get.

He and Jameson had both tuned in on her thoughts as soon as they crossed the threshold because something about the playroom had sent all Kit's mind link shields into tatters and everything she'd been thinking had suddenly been theirs for the taking. Trev was glad they had blindfolded her even though it didn't appear it had been necessary because they sure as hell hadn't concealed the location of the room. But it made it easier for them to use hand signals and when Trev looked up at Jameson, he noted his brother's expression reflected his own sense of wonder. How they'd managed to neglect her so much that she had found time to wonder this far inside the bowels of the estate was incredible and now Trev wondered what other interesting things she had discovered.

CHAPTER SEVEN

WHILE TREV TOOK care of Kit's hair, Jameson stepped in front of her and licked around and around her nipples in slow torturous circles, stopping every few rounds to blow a puff of cool air over the tightly peaked buds. "You know, my lovely mate, we have been waiting for these beauties to become available to us again." Jameson could smell her arousal and knew if he ran his fingers between her legs he would find her soaking wet. Watching her breasts swell under his touch brought a sense of satisfaction Jameson found hard to describe. Knowing that his mate found pleasure in his touch and fulfillment in his domination was pulling the beast in him closer to the surface with each passing moment. "What is your safe word, kitten?"

"Red, sir." Her voice was already filled with lust and Jameson could hardly wait to begin.

'Are you ready? Hold her hands, I'm going to clamp these little beauties.' Trev had already tied off the leather at the bottom of the braid and Jameson watched as his brother slowly slid his hands over Kit's shoulders and followed a slow sensual press of flesh against flesh until his hands shackled their mate's wrists. Just that simple act of restraint caused an audible catch in Kit's breathing causing Trev to smile over her shoulder. Jameson could hear his brother speaking softly against her ear.

"Baby, I know you don't consider this punishment, but I assure you it is coming. And when your sweet body is desperate for release and it's just a half of a heartbeat out of your reach remember why you are being denied."

Jameson found himself growling in agreement at Trev's words because they perfectly echoed his own sentiments even though he probably wouldn't have phrased it nearly so eloquently. But knowing she had not been satisfied and had hidden that fact by basically lying about it brought his mind back to what they'd planned for her. Slipping his hand into his pocket as he closed his teeth tight enough over the tight bud of her nipple, Jameson pulled back enough to make her gasp before letting it pop free. He immediately slipped the tension clamp over her nipple and smiled when she moaned softly. "We'll see how long that sweet moan lasts, love, because I'm going to tighten this up a bit because I don't believe it is quite living up to its potential just yet." Then he started slowly turning the small black cylinder at the base of the clamp and watched as the pulse at the base of her neck kicked into high gear.

As wolf shifters, their hearing was keener than that of their human counterparts so Jameson knew that Trev was also able to hear the slightest changes in Kit's body, and right now his brother had his lips pressed against the pulse point below her ear so he was no doubt hearing and feeling her blood being pumped frantically through her veins. When Kit finally cried out Jameson backed the cylinder off just the slightest bit so she was left panting as she tried to move past the pain into the pleasure she knew waited on the other side. They had only used clamps a couple of times and then they hadn't used anything with quite this much *bite*, but she had more than earned this. Just before she started to work through the haze of pain, Jameson repeated the entire process on her other nipple and this time her scream echoed off the stone walls just before her knees folded.

"Oh, my naughty little mate, stand right back up here and take your punishment like a good girl. We have decorations for these lovely chains you know. Lovely diamonds because I do believe I have heard you mention how fond you are of them." With that quick warning, Jameson clipped the extenders with the large stones they had chosen at the very tips of the chains so they would swing freely with each breath Kit took. He'd been careful when he'd attached them to keep them still, but as soon as they were in place he flicked them both at the same time with his fingers so they started swinging, and he smiled as her entire body went rigid just before she started trembling.

This time Trev growled as he bit down on the tender spot where her shoulder and neck met, "If you come without permission, mate, it will be the last release you get for the rest of the night so you better pull yourself right back from that ledge. I believe you have a punishment to get out of the way before you get a reward."

"Oh God, if this isn't the punishment I'm in...fuck a duck in a big yellow truck I...I don't..." Trev made sure she didn't have to finish the sentence because the swats he landed on each ass cheek had definitely been meant as punishment and they had their intended effect. "God damn it to hell, Trev, that fucking hurt you asshole." It took everything in him not to laugh as Jameson watched Kit's mouth fall open when she realized what she'd said. *Oh my love, you have played right into our hands.*

KIT HAD BEEN so lost in everything happening to her that she had barely registered Trev's admonishment to not come until one of them gave her permission. But the blistering swats he'd given her had pulled her back from the edge and then some. And it had been the denial of pleasure more than the pain that had rocketed her from arousal to anger and the words had flown out of her mouth before she'd had a prayer of calling them back. The men's reaction had been immediate and before she had even had a chance to apologize she found herself bent over a cool leather padded device that she knew was the spanking bench she had seen earlier. With an almost technical efficiency the men worked together to secure her to the device. Kit had been floating in a strange place between fear and anticipation and hadn't taken stock of just how vulnerable everything was until one of the men walked behind her, and just that small movement of air drifting over her soaking wet pussy caused her to jerk against the restraints.

She realized that every inch of her pussy was spread wide for their view and use, and her rear star was also nicely peaked and spread open as well. The padded board pressing between her breasts kept her from folding in two, but the semicircular cuts allowed her breasts to move freely. Even the smallest sway set the chins dangling from the nipple clamps swinging so the weight of the diamonds Jameson had attached were tugging against her tender flesh. Hell, even breathing was lancing white hot sparks of need through her entire body. Each one of those sparks faded into pure need that was quickly moving from a dull throbbing ache to a renewal of the soul deep connection that she had longed to feel again, that driving need to submit and feel safe in their love and care. The promises of the sexual sea that she could just fall into beckoned and she responded because she knew Jameson and Trev would catch her. She didn't have to be the responsible one, the daughter, granddaughter, employee, friend, wife, or mother. All she had to do was submit and let them lead her to the release that right now looked like a very small light at the end of a very long tunnel.

The first crack of the wooden paddle over ass cheeks was more of a surprise than true pain and Kit shrieked in response. Jameson's words caused her focus to zero in on his words and off the flames dancing over her ass. "Why are you being punished, mate?" Kit knew he had called her mate rather than kitten or love on purpose and the fact that he was deliberately drawing attention to that *distance* made her sad even as she recognized the manipulation.

"I faked an orgasm." She barely leashed in the rest of the comment because adding "I knew your ego wouldn't appreciate knowing how unsatisfying our sex life had become" wasn't likely to win her any Dale Carnegie awards for making friends and influencing people.

"And?" This time it was Trev's growled words that sounded in her ear.

"Ummm, I don't really know anything else. And in all honesty, I have been trying to tell you that I wanted to go back to the way things were and you just kept blowing me off." Kit felt both men go still and she wondered if they really believed that she really was such a coward that she wouldn't have addressed the issue.

Kit finally felt the air around her stirring and then the blindfold was pulled up so she was left blinking against the light even though the room itself was actually fairly dim. Trev was leaning down on one knee and gently stroking his fingers along the bottom side of her jaw. "Explain," was all he said, but she understood immediately that they hadn't heard anything she'd said these past several weeks and that hurt her far worse than any punishment they could met out.

"Did you really think I would just fake my satisfaction the first time I felt like I'd been left at the edge of a release that I knew would only strengthen our bond?" There was a part of her that was angry because they'd assumed she was that incredibly selfish and deceitful, but there was a larger part that now understood just how little they knew about each other. Their relationship had gone from zero to full immersion in a matter of hours so it stood to reason that they would still be discovering things about each other as mates for a long time. Taking a deep breath and releasing it in a rush, Kit looked into the baffled expression on Trev's face. "I'm really sorry. I wasn't trying to be disrespectful or deceitful. I was just reaching...and trying to wish something into existence that obviously just isn't meant to be."

Kit drew in a deep breath and tried to still her galloping heart. She didn't break her gaze with Trev, nor did she try to stop the tear that now rolled silently down her cheek. She knew the only way to survive the heartache that was ahead was to step back and give her heart and mind a chance to re-group. Pulling in a deep breath and hoping she seemed more confident than she was, Kit tried to sound confident in her words, "You are punishing me for the wrong reason you know. Red."

Trevlon Wolf was rarely shocked by the actions of people around him because he was usually excellent at reading a situation and understanding exactly what was headed his way. But his mate had just completely blindsided him and from the sharp intake of breath he heard from his twin, Jameson hadn't fared any better. The wooden paddle Jameson had been holding clattered to the floor and when Trev looked up the look of devastation in his brother's eyes was haunting. People did shock Jameson on occasion because Jameson was busier with pack business, but they rarely surprised Trev the way Kit just had. Jameson didn't have the luxury of sitting to the side watching people's reactions and responses when they didn't know they were being observed the way Trev did. And Trev had always considered his ability to feed Jameson that kind of information one of his greatest contributions to their co-Alpha status.

And now Trev felt as if he'd let his brother down in a way he'd have never even considered possible. How had this gotten so far out of control? Kit's softly whispered, "Please" snapped them both into action and they had her released and standing in seconds. Trev tried to pull her into his arms and when she flinched and instinctively stepped back, his heart dropped into his stomach. Jameson had stepped over to grab the black silk robe they'd purchased for her months earlier. When he approached her, Trev watched as Kit seemed to shrink into herself as she wrapped the robe around her like a protective barrier.

'We'll give her a bit to settle but then we have to talk to her and fix this. I'll die if she leaves us,' Jameson's haunted voice filled Trev's mind.

'She isn't going to leave.'

'Brother, there are many ways to leave and they aren't all

physical.' Trev knew Jameson was right, but even thinking that they might lose Kit was more than he could even begin to process. They slowly walked Kit back to their suite of rooms and the silence that had surrounded them had been almost deafening in its significance. When they entered their suite Kit quickly disappeared into the master suite's bathroom. Trev had followed her to the door and turned to walk away to give her a little privacy when he heard the water start. But just as he started to step away, he heard soft sobs that stole his breath. Jameson was at his side in an instant, obviously he'd heard Kit as well. Trev opened the door and stepped in to find her curled in the corner of the shower. Shedding his own clothing quickly, he stepped in and pulled her up and into his arms and just held her. He'd noted the nipple clamps on the counter and the realization that she'd removed them herself without crying out, but had folded from heartache, was tearing him apart.

"Shhh, baby. You are going to make yourself sick." Tracing rune protection symbols over her slender back as he slowly moved them both under one of the shower's large rain showerheads, he whispered against her ear, "Remember our first night together when I traced those symbols on you?" When she nodded, he continued, "I was so impressed when you recognized them. I felt like my mom had sent me a special nod of approval from the other side. That it was a message from her telling me 'yes...you've finally found her. This is *the one*'. It was one of those moments in your life that you never forget...one of those rare ones that only becomes sweeter and more poignant over time."

Kit pulled back just enough for him to look down into her red-rimmed eyes. Their emerald depths were filled with apprehension and for just a moment he realized she was floundering. He had always believed that the worst thing a Dom could do to a sub was ignore them because by nature most are driven to please others so being ignored doesn't give them anything solid to hold on to. It was that moment of clarity that told him that was exactly what they'd *done*, but it didn't tell him how to repair the damage.

'*I think we need to delay the discussion we had planned, brother. Let's get her settled and then I'm calling Marcus.*' Trev just gave a short nod and they finished their showers quickly and then settled Kit into bed. They knew Kit had already made arrangements for the babies to spend the night with their nannies, and Trev was grateful when he saw how quickly she had fallen deeply asleep.

Moving downstairs, he nor Jameson talked about what had happened. By unspoken agreement, they'd kept to their own thoughts while they set up the video call with Marcus's personal assistant at The Dark Knights Club. Marcus Hines was the owner of New York's most exclusive sex club, he was also their friend and mentor. Marcus had trained both he and Jameson as Doms and they'd often sought out his help and guidance both in and out of the bedroom. Marcus had been in a twenty-four/seven Master-slave relationship with Reagan for over almost ten years and Trev knew that they had experienced more than one rough patch in the beginning. Reagan had been a fiercely independent career woman who had nearly worked herself to death trying to fill the void in her life she hadn't understood wasn't career related.

Marcus had told them that when he'd seen the petite beauty walk through the doors of the main room during one of the club's invitation only meet and greet nights, he'd felt as if he'd been struck by lightning. She had actually come in using a friend's invitation and the comedy of errors that followed had almost doused the spark they'd both felt when they'd been introduced. Both Trev and Jameson had been at Dark Knights that evening and had watched as the man they respected and had seen exhibit remarkable control in even the most difficult situations almost fold when he'd been forced to punish the little party crasher. But remarkably it hadn't frightened her away, she'd told them all later it had been like a veil had lifted and for the first time in years she had felt whole.

Trev knew that calling Marcus meant they'd be getting Reagan's input as well, because they were rarely separated for longer than a few hours at a time and at this time of day, she would most definitely be within a few feet of her Master. She wouldn't answer any questions or contribute until Marcus gave her the go ahead, but then she'd speak openly and honestly. Reagan had worked part time for several years, but as soon as her Master noticed even the slightest symptom of burn out, he reined her in. Over the years she'd cut back so now she worked just enough to keep her credentials as a child psychologist current. The last Trev had heard the book Reagan had written was scheduled for publication sometime this coming summer. And now, Trev found himself sitting on the edge of his seat hoping like hell their friends would be able to give them some kind of guidance because he could almost feel the life he'd thought they had been building slipping through his fingers.

CHAPTER EIGHT

J AMESON SAT IN front of the screen and explained everything to Marcus and Reagan giving them every detail he
could remember. Trev had filled in a lot of blanks and
when they'd finished Marcus hadn't said anything for
several long seconds. His friend was sitting in his office but
was using the new conferencing equipment he'd recently
installed so he could conduct meetings without Reagan
being forced to kneel behind his desk. As usual, she was
naked at his feet but she wasn't really kneeling in her usual
slave pose, which was highly unusual.

Marcus Hines was not only one of the best Dominants
and Dom trainers Jameson had ever met, he was also a
gifted empath and psychic. When Jameson realized he'd
been staring at Reagan as he puzzled over her unusual
posture he quickly returned his eyes to his friend. Marcus
chuckled at what Jameson was sure his guilt-ridden
expression. "You know that I never mind you or Trevlon
looking at my pet. She is beautiful and I'm very proud of
her. But in answer to your questions, yes she is in a much
different pose and for a very good reason." Marcus turned
his attention to Reagan, "Stand up, pet, it is time to show
off a bit." Even through the camera her blush was a lovely
deep pink.

They watched as Marcus did something they had rarely
seen him do before, he stood and gently pulled his petite

slave to her feet. It was instantly obvious that Reagan was pregnant although Jameson had no idea how far along she might be. "Congratulations to you both. You're going to be wonderful parents. When is she due, Marcus?" Trev asked.

Marcus pulled her on to his lap and she curled into him like the well-satisfied pet she was. "Just two months to go. She has been working very hard to stay in shape and I'm very proud of her efforts, but she'll be cutting back on those workouts now that I've found out just how intense they have been. As you'll notice," suddenly the camera was lowering and zooming in on Reagan's very red ass, "she has been given quite a paddling for not taking care of herself. But I do believe she sees it differently now, don't you, pet?" Trev and Jameson laughed at her quietly spoken agreement.

Marcus looked at them both thoughtfully before speaking. "As to your problem with Kathleen, I'm actually quite disappointed in the both of you. I know for a fact I trained you better than this. Think back on the time between her mental admission, which you really didn't have a right to even know, and the moment she used her safe word. Did you at any time talk with her about why she had thought faking a release was the right thing to do? Had she previously been told that it was against the rules? Because as I recall she was a total BDSM novice when you married and collared her and with everything that has happened...are you certain you have really *trained her as a sub*? Or perhaps you just assumed you could waver from play to vanilla without some sort of signal to let her know when or why you are changing the game plan? Because even long term D/s couples have those signals firmly in place."

Jameson thought back and groaned when he started tallying up all the mistakes they'd made. Marcus's amused voice sounded over their speakers, "Aww, you're seeing the mistakes you made, aren't you? And let's consider how many of those were made because your pride had been wounded?" Jameson didn't even want to admit that Marcus's words were true even when it was blatantly obvious that they were.

"And Trevlon, where were you when this was going down like the Titanic? You are the *watcher*, I strongly suspect it's a natural tendency and a role you have filled since childhood. But this time, it appears that all you did was throw gas on the fire." Marcus paused and shook his head like a teacher who was being forced to deal with students who hadn't properly prepared for an exam—which wasn't all that far off the mark.

"If you are going to have a successful ménage relationship, you do indeed have to work as a team so your submissive doesn't play you against one another. But that being said, either one of you should always be ready to step in when ego and pride are driving a scene. If *anything* other than meeting the needs of the submissive is the impetus of what you are doing, then you are doing it for the wrong reasons. And I assure you, from what I'm hearing, meeting Kathleen's needs was not at all what was driving that scene. And did you say that you left an untrained sub blindfolded during a punishment scene?"

When both he and Trevlon nodded numbly, Marcus continued, "So you couldn't really properly monitor the situation because you couldn't see into your subs eyes, what you know is *always* your best line of assessment. And unfortunately, Trevlon, you didn't step in until this whole thing was so far gone it was irrecoverable." The silence that followed was crushing and Jameson knew that Marcus was just letting them consider all the wrong turns they'd taken before he helped them—at least Jameson hoped like hell they'd be able to fix the problem.

Jameson watched as Reagan twinged and then shifted ever so slightly in Marcus's lap. That break in position was something he'd never seen her do before and he knew the muscle spasm must have been extremely painful for her to show any outward sign of discomfort. "Excuse me for just a moment, gentlemen, my pet needs my attention for a bit." Marcus stood smoothly and Jameson admired how easily he handled her despite what appeared to be at least a fifteen-year age difference. Most people wouldn't ever guess how old Marcus was because he'd always kept himself physically fit, and Jameson knew that his friend had intensified his workouts after turning fifty last year. Even though he'd seemed good-natured about his inner circle's teasing about the milestone, Jameson had known it was a bigger issue for him than Marcus had been willing to admit.

Marcus walked back into view escorting Reagan who was now wearing one of Marcus's dress shirts that dwarfed her. "I forget that Reagan's muscles don't like being in one position for too long. Now, I'd like to include her in our conversation if you don't mind. As you know she usually works with kids but I'm sure some of the information will cross over and her experience as a newbie thrust into the deep-end of the lifestyle will be valuable."

"Absolutely. Reagan, we'd be interested in knowing what you think. Any suggestions as to how to repair the damage we've done?" Trev had moved in closer so Reagan would be able to see him as well as hear him speak. They had both enjoyed the conversations they'd had with her, and knew how witty and insightful she was. Reagan and Marcus had a very intense relationship, and it was far more structured around the lifestyle than Jameson or Trev were interested in living, but it seemed to work for them.

"You have already been over the missteps so I won't review those." She smiled at them warmly and added, "Besides, I'm sure you are more interested in solutions than rehashing all of those points. But I want you to remember, if you are still *there* in your mind, you won't be *here*. And that, my friends, will make all the difference between your success and failure in any attempt at reparation, so keep that point in mind."

Their expressions must have given away their confusion because Marcus barked out his laughter. "Pet, you better rein in the doctor-speak a bit." Then directing his comments to them, he added, "She is telling you to stop beating yourselves up over it. You can't keep thinking about all the ways you've managed to fuck this up—despite the fact it's actually a fairly impressive number."

Reagan smiled gently even as she started to roll her eyes before catching herself and grinning. "What my Master is not saying very tactfully is correct. Your focus needs to be on Kit. She is lovely and really wants to do well, but she is very new to the lifestyle despite the fact you have been mated for over a year. During that time, you haven't followed D/s rules per se and she hasn't spent much time at all with other submissives so she hasn't even had the chance to observe."

She paused for several seconds to let her words sink in, and Jameson smiled as he returned his attention to her and saw her smiling indulgently. The patient, observant doctor persona was present, but her eyes were alight with friendship as well and Jameson found it oddly comforting.

"The key to all of this is listening to her. So many people ask the right questions, but then they don't actually listen to the answers. And I also encourage you to use the active listening skills I know you have learned as Dominants. Reflect the answers back to her to ensure you are *hearing* what she actually intended to convey. And the conversation should really take place on neutral ground." When he started to speak she held up her hand, "I know that is difficult because of the threats she had gotten in the past, perhaps just having neutral people present might help. So how about this? What if Master Marcus and I came out to visit? I haven't seen the babies for too long and maybe Kit would benefit from some girl time."

Jameson was equally touched and relieved by her suggestion and they'd quickly made arrangements for the Hines to join them the next evening for dinner. After disconnecting the call, Jameson leaned back into his chair and looked over at his brother. Trev seemed lost in thought and Jameson knew his brother was feeling guilty for his part in everything that had happened earlier with Kit. Ordinarily Trev was the more sensitive of the two of them and the fact that he hadn't tuned in to their mate was going to be difficult for him to overcome. "Reagan is right you know. We can't wallow in the mistakes we've made— and God knows there have been plenty! And they started the first night we met her."

Jameson would never forget seeing Kit for the first time. She'd been standing in line to get into their club and his eyes had been drawn to her, first by her long flowing red hair, but then it had been something else. Try as he had, he'd never been able to put his finger exactly on what had kept him from being able to look away from her. When he'd seen she was ready to enter the club, he'd found himself walking down the stairs into the open bar and dance area, and his fate had been sealed in an instant.

While on the stairs, he'd been hit with the scent of his

mate and had become single-minded in his quest of conquer and claim. And now, looking back it was embarrassing to admit just how little finesse had been involved. He and Trev had traveled all over the world looking for their mate, and after their third overseas trip they had finally decided they had little choice but to let the fates provide when they were ready. So when Kathleen Harris had walked onto their life's stage just a few short weeks later, the Alpha pack leader in him had clawed its way front and center.

Shaking his head as if that action alone could clear his distracted thinking, Jameson turned to Trev. "We'll eat outside tomorrow night. The ambiance will be good for both little subs and it looked like Reagan could use a bit of pampering as well so we'll make sure there are soft pillows for the chairs."

Trev chuckled, "Yeah, those handprints on her ass were pretty well defined. Pretty easy to see that Marcus was none too happy about her workouts. Hell's fire, his workouts rivals the training of most Olympic athletes so I have to wonder what on earth she'd been doing to prompt that reaction." Jameson laughed at his brother's observation because it was so accurate.

Shoving to his feet, Jameson started for the door. "Let's go take care of our mate. I believe we need to start from the beginning in more ways than one and I'll try to hold my bruised ego in check this time." *Never in my wildest imagination could I have imagined making so many mistakes with someone so important.*

66

CHAPTER NINE

K IT'S MIND WAS floating between the fogginess of sleep and being fully awake but the faint sound of a baby's cry was pulling her closer to the surface. Rolling toward the edge of the bed without even opening her eyes, she came up against an immovable wall of warm flesh and instantly relaxed in Jameson's arms. She didn't need to see her mates to tell them apart, their scents alone revealed who she was pressed against. "Good afternoon, love." Jameson's words were warm and moist against her ear and sent shivers of anticipation and desire all the way down her spine. *Wait. Did he say afternoon? Holy shit.* Thoughts were suddenly racing through Kit's mind at warp speed and as she struggled to sit upright, his arm tightened around her waist like a steel band. "Stop. You are just fine where you are and our sweet babies are being well cared for. Well...they are likely being spoiled rotten, but they are definitely being well tended."

"But you said afternoon and I can't believe I slept so long. What on earth is everyone going to think of me? I am not lazy and this is unforgiveable. I have children to care for and—" Jameson cut her off with a kiss. She had actually forgotten about the events of the evening before until he reached around her and squeezed one of the very tender spots on her ass. She might not have gotten much of the punishment they had been planning to met out, but what little she'd gotten had been extremely effective. When she flinched Jameson pulled back and looked into her eyes.

"We're having guests for dinner tonight, kitten. Marcus and Reagan will be here at eight. Trev and I have planned something special for you this afternoon. But first we need to get you up and dressed because your granny is here." He must have sensed her hesitance because he quickly added, "No, we did not call her and no your mother is not with her." She let out a breath she didn't even know she was holding and he chuckled. "We do want to talk about how things went last night, but I want you to know Trev and I are taking full responsibility for that cluster fuck and we want to set things right. You were right to call an end to the scene, kitten. And from the bottom of my heart I'm sorry for not listening. Communication is the foundation of all marriages and with all of the special circumstances surrounding ours it's even more important." His knuckles were trailing down the sides of her face and she realized she was pressing into his touch. His fingers clasped her chin as he brought her focus to his face. "You are not just our wife and mate, kitten. You are our world, and we have handled things very badly. Trev and I both know we'll make mistakes again, but we won't make this one again. Let us make it up to you."

Kit was shocked to her core by his admission. She knew that as the Wolf Pack's Alpha, Jameson was accustomed to being followed and obeyed in all things. She also noted that he hadn't used his compelling voice, which she knew was his way of making sure her decision was made of her own free will. And while she loved the show of respect, she also missed her Dom, the one who listened to not only her words, but also her body. She missed the man who hadn't taken no for an answer the first night they'd met as he led her to his office to meet his brother. And her heart ached for the man who didn't treat her like she was made of glass. And even though that wasn't the man lying next to her asking for a second chance, she held out hope she'd be able to find him again. And if there was anyone who could help, it would be Marcus Hines.

She'd only spoken with Marcus and Reagan a few times at various events, but she knew both Jameson and Trev considered Marcus one of their closest friends. She also knew Marcus had trained them as Doms so it was interesting that he was coming to dinner. There was an air of familiarity surrounding Marcus that she hadn't been able to identify, but the strange feeling hadn't seemed threatening, so Kit had let it go.

Kit had instantly liked Reagan even though she didn't completely understand the other woman's choices. After all, she'd given up an extremely lucrative practice as a psychologist to become a sex slave to the city's most well-known sexual dominant. Kit knew Reagan still did volunteer work to keep her certifications current and that she'd been writing a book, so she was anxious to catch up and maybe steel away for a little girl chat.

Kit finally realized that she hadn't answered Jameson's question and she felt guilty for having put that hesitance in his eyes. She leaned forward and kissed him sweetly, "I love you and I'm sorry I messed up so badly. I really didn't understand all the implications and I was just kind of going off all the stuff I've read in magazines. Please don't be angry." Kit knew her eyes had filled with tears and that her voice had gotten impossibly soft, but at least she'd gotten the words out and that was really all she had been able to hope for.

KIT HAD QUICKLY stunned him with her apology and then she'd scrambled over him and hurried into the bathroom. She'd been gone before he'd even processed her words and he'd shaken his head at how often she was able to surprise him. Since he was already dressed, Jameson headed downstairs. When he opened the door of the office he shared with Trev he was surprised to see Ruby Stone standing with her back to him looking out of the enormous curved glass window overlooking the forest that surrounded the estate. He hadn't made any noise but she'd heard him enter. "Good afternoon, Jameson. I assume Trevlon will be here shortly?" Jameson didn't know where Trev was but before he could explain that to the tiny witch, the side office door opened and Trev stepped through.

"You called me?" Trev's question had been directed at Jameson, but quickly switched his attention to Ruby when he heard her giggle just before her red sequined high tops danced a quick jig.

"Damn, I'm good. And that isn't some easy parlor trick I'll tell you for sure. You two have that mind link thing locked up like the damned crown jewels, but I managed to wiggle in just a bit. And no, I don't want to use it often because it would be just too much information for me. But I really needed to speak with you both before Kit comes down."

They all settled on the leather wingback chairs facing the fireplace and Ruby didn't waste any time getting straight to the point. "The latest threat to Kit and the children didn't actually come from Damian. Even though it sounded to her as if it was him it was actually his much less powerful brother Devin." Jameson watched as the little bundle of energy bounced out of her chair and started pacing the exact path her granddaughter had walked last night. "Devin's main claim to fame is his brother. And the only reason he is really a threat is because he is a spineless minion of his brother and he is blindly loyal. Damian isn't recovered yet, but he is able to speak from the other side of the seals we've placed over the portals so he's directing Devin's actions."

"Hold on, Ruby. I'm afraid we need to backtrack a bit. How did he get back behind the seals? And where are these portals?" Jameson knew he'd asked the same questions Trev had been considering.

"See, that's part of what made this so puzzling. No one could figure out how Kit was able to send him back behind the seals and I'm convinced that she doesn't know either. The only answer we have at this point is that the surge of power she used was available because she was able to draw power from the twins she was carrying." She held up her hand when they started to speak. "Hear me out. I realize that she was barely pregnant, but the moment of conception is all it takes when we are dealing with magical ability of this magnitude. Quite frankly, I think this is proof of just how powerful her magic is. The Supreme Council is watching this whole thing very closely because fated magic like Kit's is extremely rare, coming along perhaps once or twice every century. The Council sent me here to step up Kit's training because without clear direction, magic as powerful and unfocused as hers can easily cause a lot of collateral damage. Also, we have reason to believe Damian is asking Devin to bring Kit to one of the portals so she can free him."

"She would never do that." Trev had bolted to his feet

and Jameson could feel the outrage pulsing through his brother.

Ruby smiled in understanding and moved to stand in front of Trev. She placed her small wrinkled hand on his chest as she spoke, "Trevlon, what would you do to save the lives of your children? What would you do to save Kit's life? Anything? Everything?"

Jameson watched as his brother seemed to melt back into his chair. "You're right. I know you are. But I also know Kit and just being placed in that position is going to break her heart." Jameson agreed with Trev but as usual, his focus was more on what they could do to prevent her being faced with such a gut wrenching decision.

"I see the questions in your eyes, Jameson, and that is exactly why I'm here. I spoke with the staff earlier and they told me about your plans for Kit this afternoon and this evening. I'm looking forward to resting and then playing with my great-grandchildren a bit. Traveling isn't as easy as it used to be and I want to be well rested when Kit and I get to work. We'll be spending a lot of time in that lovely lab you made for her, that place is sweet indeed."

Jameson couldn't hold back his burst of laughter at Ruby's slang and he laughed again when she actually blushed. "What? I hear the young people say that all the time. I used it right, I know I did." Ruby seemed frustrated with their amusement and looked like a petulant child. Jameson wondered if she would stomp her foot if he didn't smooth over his faux pas.

"You did indeed use it perfectly, Ruby. It was just a surprise although I'm not sure why." He took a good look at her attire and laughed again. The woman was always colorful, both in her personality and the way she dressed. But in all honesty, today she looked like she'd been dressed by the Shriner's. Her bright red sequined high tops were accented with purple socks and a denim skirt with sunshine yellow leather trim. Her blouse was a vibrant orange he was sure would glow in the dark and he'd seen her lime-green leather jacket laying over the back of the sofa when he came in. One thing was for certain, their children were going to love her.

CHAPTER TEN

T REV HAD SUPERVISED Kit's spa afternoon from afar...mostly. He hadn't been able to resist watching the waxing session because the camera had afforded him a perfect view of her sweet pink pussy. With her friend Libby's help, they'd managed to arrange for her to enjoy all her favorite clinicians within the safety of the estate's mansion. And the result had been well worth the effort because she had emerged from the makeshift spa smiling from ear to ear. She looked incredible with her hair cut and styled and her face glowing after the skin treatments. But it had been the smile that had been shining from the inside out that had been what caught his eye. He'd asked them to call him a few minutes before she was finished so he'd been leaning against the wall in the hallway when she walked out. She'd taken one look at him and leapt into his waiting arms.

"Thank you. You have no idea what a wonderful surprise this was. I feel ever so much better and the timing is perfect since we're having guests." When he'd pressed his lips to hers he had intended for it to be a quick peck, but the minute her soft lips opened and he tasted her, he was lost.

Turning so her back was pressed against the wall, he plundered her mouth with his. The short white silk robe she was wearing tied in the front, so he was able to quickly pull the two sides apart and bare her bountiful breasts to his view. "Fuck, you get more gorgeous by the day. And you are all mine at this moment, baby." He easily wrapped his arm around her and drew his fingers through her wet folds. Sighing, he leaned his forehead against hers and just let the joy of the moment move over him. She'd wrapped her legs around him and it left her open to his questing fingers, and he was happy to take advantage of her open position. Pushing his fingers into her channel, he smiled at how wet she was already and he'd barely begun. Kissing his way around to her ear, he whispered, "You're so wet for me, baby. I can't tell you how much that pleases me. The sweet musk of your arousal fills the air around us and my body is fighting against the sweet temptation to fuck you right against this wall."

Kit moaned and he followed his words up with a small bite to the lobe of her ear. "I don't want to leave you wanting, baby. Hang on to my shoulders and let me give you what you need." She squirmed against his touch and he set a quick pace with his fingers, fucking them in and out with just enough curve that she would be able to hear just how wet she was. He felt her muscles start to tense and then flutter around his fingers and he knew she was getting close. "Give it to me, baby. Come on my fingers."

He'd barely caught her scream in his kiss as she let go. Her entire body was shaking with the intensity of her climax and he just kept pushing in and out so when she was just beginning to descend from the peak, he shifted the angle just enough that he pressed against her g-spot. The change ramped her straight back up and over into another release, this one even stronger than the first.

When she finally sagged limply in his arms, gasping for breath, Trev felt a sense of satisfaction move over him. Just knowing he could still have that profound effect on his mate filled him with hope. Despite Jameson's fear that she might withdraw from them, Trev didn't think it was what she wanted. No, he was betting that any emotional distance she managed to place between them was more about protecting herself than it was about her mates not being what she needed.

"I love you. I just wanted to tell you because, well...I messed up so bad yesterday and I haven't really had a chance to apologize to you yet." Trev pulled back from her so he could look into her emerald eyes that were bright and shining with unshed tears.

"Baby, I'll love you until my last breath and nothing you can ever do will change that. And if it takes me until that moment to make you believe what I've told you, then so be it." He paused so she could think about what he'd said before speaking again. "I know you and Jameson had this conversation this morning, so you already know that we are the ones to blame for the way things went down. We haven't been good Doms, and probably haven't even been particularly attentive mates. But we'll be working to remedy that I assure you."

He set her on her feet and then caught her when her knees folded. She smiled up at him and again the beast in him wanted to howl in satisfaction. He picked her up and started up the stairs. "Trev, I can walk. I was just a bit unsteady at first. I'm too heavy to carry so far."

Is she kidding? She hasn't been eating well for quite a while from the feel of her in my arms. Further proof that they hadn't been paying her the proper amount of attention. No doubt Marcus would take one look at her and know immediately. Suddenly Trev felt like a student who was about to get a very poor report card.

THEIR DINNER HAD been relaxed and the ambiance of the back terrace had been perfect. Kit had been thrilled to find out Reagan was expecting and they'd spent most of the meal chatting about babies. Marcus hadn't let one moment go by that he wasn't studying both women intently, and yet he hadn't missed a beat of his conversation with Trev and Jameson either. Trev found himself listening to the women and heard them wondering if they would be allowed to walk through the gardens. Marcus leaned forward and slid a finger along the top edge of Reagan's diamond collar. "Yes, my pet. Go for a walk, but stay within my sight. I take good care of what belongs to me and I want to be sure you are safe at all times." Marcus leaned down and kissed her slightly rounded belly. "Take good care of your mama."

Trev and Jameson both kissed Kit soundly and cautioned her to stay where they could see her as well. Trev was glad they'd let her wear a more conservative dress because she had seemed much more settled when she found out she didn't have to eat naked. The last time they'd met Marcus and Reagan for a meal it had been at a club function and both women had spent the entire evening naked despite the fact Kit had been almost three months pregnant. She had been royally steamed, but had quieted down her protests after they'd warmed her ass up right in the middle of the room.

"She's terrified of displeasing you and that annoys her." Marcus hadn't wasted any time getting to the point after the women had walked away. And Trev could almost feel the smack-down coming. "She has been an independent woman for a *very long time* and discovering her submissive tendencies works against that hard won independence in her view. You haven't shown her the freedom she can find in submission. Honestly, if you two were attending the club regularly and made these mistakes, I'd send your asses straight back through the beginners Dom training." And there it was, the slap he knew they'd earned, but he hated none the less. Trev battled to keep his expression blank as he fought an internal battle wanting to justify their actions and the louder voices that acknowledged their culpability.

"And now, tell me about the magic that circles within her. She is quite powerful, you know, but it's unbridled and that is very dangerous." Marcus's voice had changed from annoyance to full blown curiosity, and Jameson marveled at his ability to switch gears so seamlessly. Out of the corner of his eye, Jameson caught a glimpse of red sequins just before Ruby seemed to materialize out of the hedge behind Trevlon.

Always the gentleman, Marcus was on his feet before either of the other men. Ruby looked at him and smiled. "Oh, you are still a charmer I see. And I, for one, am not immune, but then you already know that, don't you, Marcus?" Ruby's tone was pleasant but Jameson had definitely heard the steel band of tension threaded in her words.

"Ruby, it's nice to see you again, it's been a very long time. What brings you to the Wolf Estate? Business or pleasure?"

'How on earth do these two know each other?' Trev asked Jameson.

'No clue, brother, but I have a feeling they aren't all that close, if you know what I mean?'

"You two can stop that, you know. We can both hear

you. And to answer your question, Ruby and I were once friends a very long time ago. But she's still holding a grudge over a perceived slight." Trev knew that Marcus was speaking to them, but he'd never taken his eyes off Ruby.

"We were neighbors and the slight you refer to is the fact that you ignored my advice and people were hurt. But that was a very long time ago. What interests me now is how you figured it out? How did you know the prophecy was speaking of Jameson and Trevlon Wolf?" This was a side of Ruby Stone that Jameson had never seen, and he suddenly found himself quite interested in her story.

Marcus's first reaction was stunned, wide-eyed silence, but it was quickly replaced by a roar of laughter. "That is your first question? Oh Lord of the Light, you are jealous because you think I figured it out before you did? Is that it?" Marcus shook his head and reached for Ruby, and despite her obvious reluctance, she let the man pull her against his chest. "Well, let me put your worries to rest. I'm not the one who figured it out. It was actually your Charles. He was quite brilliant that way, you know. And not long before he died he called me and we met at a small diner. We talked for hours. Of course I had always known that the mystic's prophesy was likely speaking of Kit. What I didn't know was that the shifters were the same brothers who had become my protégé and friends. I swear the Master Planner is something to behold. We each had different pieces of the puzzle but failed to work together to solve it." He turned his gaze to Jameson and Trev, "This is why I have always told you, there are no coincidences. I had already known you for several years when Charles told me how you fit into the larger picture."

Ruby looked stunned by Marcus's revelation and Jameson hated the way she'd seemed to shrink right before his eyes. "Why didn't he tell me?" Ruby's question had been whispered in a shaky voice of a woman who felt betrayed, and Marcus didn't waste any time moving back so he was standing in front of her and clasping her small trembling hands in his much larger ones.

"He died before he could. You were gone when he talked to me. And he was already in the hospital before you got home." She seemed to sag with relief, and he smiled. "And you...you ornery old woman, if you would have returned my calls I'd have been able to tell you all of this earlier." He grinned and pulled her close. When he finally set her back at arm's length, he asked, "How is Braden? I've been so worried about him."

Jameson and Trev stood to the side completely stunned by what was being played out in front of them. There were so many questions that he didn't even know where to begin. A brilliant flash of light just to the edge of the gardens caught his attention just before a woman's shrill squeal filled the air.

CHAPTER ELEVEN

KIT AND REAGAN walked away from their men and down through the gardens. The scent of summer flowers filled the air. Stopping to admire the Gerbera daisies and New Guinnea impatiens, which were her favorites, Kit couldn't help but laugh at the wild color arrangements. "When the gardeners started working this spring, I asked them to make the gardens bright and colorful. And when I mentioned that I really hate rows of color their faces lit up as if I had just handed them a golden ticket into Willie Wonka's factory." Trailing her fingers absently along the edge of one of the large blossoms, she added, "And it seems letting them unleash some of their creativity was a great decision because the gardens have been a masterpiece of color the entire season."

Kit turned to Reagan and noticed that the professional had surfaced and seemed to be studying Kit rather than the flowers. "You are right, they are lovely. But you're stalling and I'm wondering why. You know the men won't leave us to our own devices for long, so let's get to whatever is going to help you before we stray into this fascinating exploration of horticulture. Let's see how I can help, shall we?" Kit knew she must have appeared really surprised because the other woman chuckled. "Sorry about that, old habits die hard. And now that I am only working bare bones hours, I find myself having to make the most of each minute that I'm at the clinic. I guess that mindset sort of bled over into this conversation." Reagan's shrug belied the fact that Kit could see she really did want to help and for the first time in a long while, Kit giggled at the absurdity that always seemed to surround her.

"I know that you are aware of all the ways Jameson, Trev, and I are special." Reagan nodded and Kit shook her head. "Well as if being a witch and a shifter wasn't enough to complicate things, I fall for twin shifters who are the Alphas of their pack as well as sexual Dominants. Magic's dark side is trying to recruit me, they want to claim my infants as their own, we are now sheltering a young wizard that is also a target, and my mother is a pain in my ass. And do you know what problem has all of my focus? The fact that my Doms have been playing too nice. How crazy is that?" Kit had heard her own voice raising in pitch even though she hadn't been speaking loud for fear she'd be overheard. Her heart was racing and she'd felt nearly frantic to get the information all out before she thought better of it and changed her mind.

Kit had never seen Reagan be anything but perfectly poised, so she was shocked when the woman looked at her and laughed. "Damn, girlfriend, were you afraid you weren't going to get that all out before I ran screaming into the night?"

That seemed to break the ice and they both collapsed on to a nearby bench in a fit of giggles. Several seconds and many tears later, Kit went on, "You are probably right. I really can't imagine normal humans being able to grasp all of this. And you're a psychologist so truthfully, I'm just kind of relieved that you haven't called 911 yet."

"Well, first of all, my Master is more than he seems to be, but that is his story to tell. And I can most generally tell the difference between delusional and desperate. Now, when did this vanilla crap start?" Kit relaxed and started explaining how everything had played out and how frustrated she'd been when her Doms had all but disappeared.

"I don't even know if they have been shifting and running. And now that I consider it, that could be part of the problem. The next full moon isn't until next week and I'm anxious for it myself because there is a special magic found in moonlight. I've had this restless energy coursing through my system that might not ease without the mystical cleansing of a moonlit run. I find myself lost in fear sometimes...it's that oppressive feeling that something big is going to happen. I find myself surrounded by this hyper-energy that just pulses all around me."

"And submitting to your Masters stills that energy, doesn't it? Is that what you are missing...the stillness submission brings to your mind?" Kit didn't even realize her eyes had filled with tears again until she felt the first one roll down her cheek. All she could do was nod her head because she really was shocked that Reagan had gotten it so perfectly right. "Have you talked to them about this? Have you ever negotiated a scene with them?"

"Negotiated? I don't understand."

"Oh brother, no wonder this is such a mess. I'll tell you what, the full explanation is too much to deal with in one night...it's actually a series of classes at the club. But I'm going to talk to my Master and see if he won't let me give you a crash course over the next couple of weeks. That way you'll understand what you are experiencing and you'll feel a lot more comfortable expressing your needs to—" Reagan's words had been cut off by a man stepping from behind the bushes on Kit's right.

Kit's first instinct was to step in front of her pregnant friend. "Ahh, Kathleen, you wound me. I'm not here to hurt my sister-in-law or her son, although whether or not my plans change depends entirely upon how cooperative you are." The hair was standing up on the back of Kit's neck and even she could see the sparkles beginning to crackle around her. She heard Reagan yelp of pain and knew she had probably been zapped. Kit's experience told her it had been little more than the same feeling one got from a spark from the static electricity that built up after walking across carpeting and then touching metal. *Did he say sister-in-law? What the fuck?*

Glancing over her shoulder, Kit muttered a quick apology and Reagan merely shrugged it off, and said, "Who is that ass hat anyway? And did you notice his eyes? He is just plain creepy. And why did he call me his sister-in-law? He's creepy *and* delusional, that's got to be it." Kit actually snorted a laugh at the absurdity of the entire situation. Here she was talking to a sex slave with a PhD about a wizard from the dark side, and Reagan's main observation was about his creepy eyes and that he'd mistaken her for a relative? *Talk about not grasping the severity of the situation.*

"Oh I grasp everything just fine. It's just that he is a minion and not even a very good one. I don't know his name, but it's obvious he is just a messenger. Geez Louise, he probably isn't even really good at that…whatcha' want to bet? I mean, look at him. No notebook or anything. I'll bet he's even forgotten why he's here."

Kit listened in stunned silence as Reagan further antagonized the man standing in front of them until his eyes went from glowing red to white hot. It wasn't long until he was literally shimmering and Kit was starting to really worry about what he might do. "Shut her up, Kathleen.

Now! Or you are both going to be sorry." His shaking was getting worse by the minute, and Kit was really getting concerned about how unstable he seemed to be.

"Poking the magical bear probably isn't that great of a plan, Reagan." Kit pitched her voice low and hoped that the man hadn't heard her.

"Him? Oh his just smoke and mirrors. I'll bet his boss didn't even give him any of the good toys to bring. And if his message was that damned important he'd be breathing it all over us with fire and brimstone special effects. Nope, Kit, you definitely only rated the B-team this time. Damn, girl, you're losing your touch."

By this time the man was literally vibrating with anger but Kit really could not hold back her snort of laughter and that was all it took. "My name is Devin and I will be back," and with a bright flash of light he was gone. Kit had squealed in surprise and then just stared at the spot where he'd been for long seconds until somewhere in the back of her mind she registered the shouts of people approaching them.

Before they were swarmed she turned to Reagan, "Fuck me! What were you thinking? How did you know he would fold?"

Reagan giggled, "Oh that was too easy. Hell a junior psych student could have played that one. He was obviously uncomfortable in the bad ass role and I just called his bluff."

"You called his bluff? Would you like to explain that statement, pet?" Kit grinned when Reagan paled. She'd been all sass with a demon, but was worried about her Master's reaction? *Talk about your rich irony.*

Chapter Twelve

D AMIAN STOOD NEXT to the ornately cast metal door of the portal and cursed the witch who had managed to seal him inside. "I still can't imagine how an untrained witch was able to fucking blow me into pieces so small I resembled fucking mist, and send me back behind these wretched seals." Taking a deep breath, he tried to pull back his frustration so he could deal with his half-witted brother. "Have you managed to get someone inside the Council Chambers yet?"

He knew by the sound of Devin's voice that he was leaning against the rock wall that bordered the sealed portal. It hadn't taken his brother long to learn that actually touching the door or the seals was a recipe for disaster. The portal itself reminded Damian of an overly large and ornately engraved man-hole cover that was embedded in a solid rock wall rather resting on a sidewalk. His brother was a pain in the ass and always had been. But Devin was the only member of Damian's family who had stood by him when he'd moved to the dark side as a young wizard. And if Devin managed to get a hold of Kathleen and her children, there would be no stopping them.

Damian knew in the beginning Devin hadn't been convinced that securing the fated witch mentioned in the prophecy would ever be possible. But as time had gone on, Damian had slowly managed to persuade him that Kathleen would do anything to protect her children and *that* was leverage they could be easily use to their advantage.

"No, but there are several young witches working for us who have applied for internships with various Council members. The scales will tip in our favor soon, you must be patient." Damian wasn't sure, but he thought he detected a bit of disinterest in Devin's voice, and that set his temper on a rolling boil.

"Are you fucking kidding me? Be patient? Easy for your incompetent ass to say when *you* aren't the one locked behind these wretched seals. Damn it all to hell. You've made several unsuccessful attempts and now everyone is watching you so closely, your every move is going to have to be coordinated down to a gnat's ass. You made too many ineffective moves too quickly. And each one was countered because *you* didn't plan them well enough."

"What are you talking about? No one could have known that Carla Harris would be downtown the day we went for Braden. We would have had to have at least a thousand people working to have swept the entire area for trace magic. And even then, she is one of the very best at covering her tracks. Hell, the woman's paranoia is legendary and you know it so get off my ass."

🐾 🐾 🐾

"*CONSECRO!*" DAMIAN'S VOICE boomed from the other side and Devin was grateful that his brother's magic wouldn't carry through the tightly shielded portal. Even though the magic was neutralized, the rage was still easy to feel, or at least it seemed that way as the force of it slammed into him.

"Talk to me, brother. I know there are details that you

have left out. Why is Braden so important?" Devin had asked this same question a hundred times, and he was getting ass-fucking tired of the same smoke and mirrors answers. Invariably, his brother would simply say that he was fated to be a powerful member of the magical community and that his ability to draw energy from those around him would make him even more useful. But Devin knew to the depths of his soul there was more to it than that, he just didn't know what the vital piece was that Damian was holding back.

"I've told you, he's powerful. Don't underestimate him. And he turns sixteen next week so the stakes will go up exponentially." Devin could practically hear his brother grinding his back teeth together in frustration. Damian was a powerful force and his power grew each time he took out another of his enemies. Devin had watched as his brother pulled the life force from his victims, and it was as terrifying as it was incredible to watch. Seeing the gray mist of a person's essence being sucked from them as if it was being vacuumed from one soul to another was a very powerful visual reminder of just how ruthless Damian could be. Every one of the men and women who had witnessed it knew exactly what awaited them if they strayed from the cause or failed to perform. Damian didn't just demand loyalty, he demanded total possession of one's soul.

Devin cursed his distraction when he heard Damian growl, "Are you fucking listening to me? I said I don't want the boy harmed, just capture him. And if you have to choose between him and Kathleen, then bring him. Because she will protect him just as she will her own children. Once he is in your care, you'll find it much easier to persuade Kathleen to come to me." Devin was convinced his brother was grossly underestimating how significant the protection was around Kathleen. Hell, he'd barely managed to project himself through the shields in the garden, and everything was locked down even tighter now.

"What is the connection between you and Marcus Hines's wife? You called her your sister-in-law, but she didn't seem to believe that. She wasn't at all frightened of me. It was as if she felt entitled to a 'free pass' or something." The woman that had been with Kathleen in the garden had not even flinched at his appearance, and that was beyond puzzling.

"She is of no consequence. But it is interesting to consider her Master may have told her more that I'd expected. Marcus is our father's bastard son." Devin rolled his eyes, because there was very little he wouldn't believe about their father. The man had been an amazingly gifted wizard, but had been more interested in bedding every woman he met than in amassing any real power and influence. Devin decided to wait until Damian continued, he was tired of operating with only half the damned information. He knew full well that if he was killed trying to help Damian, his brother wouldn't lose a moments sleep and that Devin's position would be filled within the hour. And that realization had given him pause several times lately.

"Why do you refer to him as her Master?"

"She is his sex slave. He may be the light to my dark, but his isn't a pure light either if you ask the moral majority." Devin cringed at Damian's maniacal laughter from the other side. *He's fucking losing it. Demon-mean is one thing, but an insane demon is far more dangerous.* Knowing he was already in so deep that it would be nearly impossible to get out was a sadly sobering thought.

"Light to your dark? Explain that."

"There isn't enough time for that now. Go back and bring Braden to me. And remember, I don't want him harmed." Devin could sense his brother's departure just by the shift in the air around him. Anytime Damian was near the air almost crackled around him as his energy tried to pull more from others, and Devin found it exhausting to be near him for any length of time. Every time he'd traveled through the cave to the portal, Devin felt an overwhelming pressure—as if he had a ton of rock sitting directly on his chest. And now, as he made his way back through the cave, the oppressing force was easing with each step he took away from Damian. Whether the discomfort was related to being close to his brother or to the portal leading to the dark side, was the question.

Chapter Thirteen

I T HAD BEEN almost a week since the incident in the gardens and Kit had been working diligently with her grandmother practicing her control and working to focus the energy of her magic toward a specific target. Kit knew the strength of her magic was only limited by her inability to focus, and those were the skills that she would need the most. Granny Good Witch was slowly letting loose the details of her acquaintance with Marcus, and Kit was still grappling with the fact that two men who were polar opposites shared such a close genetic link. Damn it all, just accepting that Marcus was a friend of her grandfather's had taken her several days. But Kit was certain her mates had struggled even more than she had. The revelation that their most trusted friend had kept so many secrets from them had unnerved both Jameson and Trevlon.

Marcus had assured her that her mates would eventually fully understand his reasoning. He'd even made some suggestions for Kit's magical training that her granny had reluctantly seemed to agree were helpful. Kit hated the tension that seemed to cloud their friendship now, but she had also realized it wasn't anything she could change. She'd thrown herself into her training and found that learning the spells and incantations was usually fairly easy because she'd been hearing them her entire life so her mind was already programed for them.

Kit had run almost each night, with Jameson and Trev flanking her, so she'd quickly learned all the short cuts and trails of the estate. They had worked hard to make sure she knew every nook and cranny, each hiding spot and route of escape. She tried to spend some time with Braden, but Angie and her husbands hadn't seemed too eager to share him just yet. Looking over the cluttered counter in the lab, Kit asked, "So, Granny Good Witch, what do you think is going to happen with Braden? Nick has been working with him so much in the gym I'm surprised the Olympic committee hasn't been knocking at our door."

When her grandmother looked up from the mixture she'd been stirring, Kit started giggling. Her granny looked like a crazy witch right out of some children's science storybook. Her goggles were smudged and smoke covered, her hair was standing out in every direction as if she'd encountered a bolt of lightning, which probably wasn't far from the truth, and she had a black smudge over her left cheek. Blinking her eyes in confusion at Kit's reaction, she just stared until Kit grabbed a small handheld mirror they'd used earlier and held it up for her. "Well daft...it looks like I'm channeling Albert. He really was a quirky one you know. But damn he was funny. He always regretted introducing the world to atomic power. We tried to tell him it would have happened eventually, but he never did really manage to let go of his guilt."

It had always fascinated Kit how casually her grandparents referred to historical figures. It had always humbled her how closely those who had shaped history's most important moments were linked to the magical community. "Tell me what you know about the battle that is coming." Kit watched her grandmother remove her goggles and set everything aside giving all of her attention to their conversation. Kit remembered that her grandfather had always done that...set anything he was reading or working on to the side so whoever he was talking to knew they had his complete attention. Seeing her granny do the same thing let her feel like she'd just gotten a love-sign from her grandfather, and she sent up a silent thank you for his effort.

"As I explained the other night, we know Damian is still trapped on the other side of the seals, and I can't tell you how hard I have tried to figure out exactly how you managed that feat so we could repeat it if we needed to. But anyway, we know you and Braden are central to the battle, and that is why you are both being targeted. Of course, he is the easier target because he is a still technically a child in the magical community. However, his birthday is coming up soon, and when he turns sixteen he'll come into his powers and then we are going to have a lot more to work with. You are going to see his abilities become exponentially stronger as that day approaches because he is safe and being nurtured. It's much like what we saw happen with you, even though you didn't fully come in to your powers until you were mated, we still saw huge advances in your abilities the more time you spent with your father and grandfather. They were your anchors. As shifters they are more earth bound and that grounding allowed you to pull from the earth's natural powers. It is those powers that all magic streams from. Braden's abilities will come on earlier, but he is going to have his own battles to fight." Kit had ask her granny hundreds of questions over the years and she'd always seemed to skirt around the issue. This was the first time Kit could remember her grandmother giving her a straight answer that contained valuable information.

"But what do you know about the confrontation with Damian? When will he stop trying to persuade and start being forceful? I mean, so far he hasn't seemed like a very formidable enemy, if you know what I mean."

Her granny sighed and looked up with sad eyes. "Don't underestimate him, Kathleen. He is indeed a very worthy opponent. But I don't think you will face him personally for some time." Her grandmother paused as if lost in thought and Kit was beginning to wonder if she was going to say any more when she finally began speaking again. "For now, our emphasis has to be teaching you to control and focus your energy so the magic is delivered with pinpoint accuracy exactly where you send it."

"Is this a battle I'll have to fight alone?" Suddenly the thought of relying solely on magic to defend her children, mates, and herself was scary as hell.

"No, and I hope I am still here to help. Your mother will help, and Marcus will be here as well. His insight into helping predict Damian's behavior will be extremely useful. And the Council will send others you meet as time moves along, but you'll be the focal point of their energy. In truth, part of your power is your ability to act as a conduit for the energy of others. You will be able to funnel the power of other witches and wizards surrounding you. It is the same principle as a prism. Various rays of light will go through you and come out brilliant and much more powerful. That ability is going to make the difference in the end...but it also why the dark side wants you so desperately."

Suddenly Kit was terrified she wouldn't ever be ready in time because there was so much to learn. There wasn't any reason to ask her grandmother any more questions, because even Kit knew that no one knew all the details of the future. But she did know she wasn't going to keep her own children in the dark like she had been. Perhaps if her training had started earlier she'd be more prepared now.

RUBY WATCHED THE play of emotions cross Kit's face. Carla had been wrong to keep her daughter away from the magic community until she was mated. Sure, Kit hadn't fully come into her powers until then, but she had still had enough power to begin the learning process and would have at least felt somewhat more prepared for what she was facing. But Ruby also knew that her own daughter had recognized Kit was, in all likelihood, the one the prophesy spoke of, and Carla's pride had always gotten in the way.

Kit was an incredibly bright young woman in addition to being so magically gifted, that at times, Ruby had struggled to hold back her own stunned expressions. The lovely young witch standing across the counter from her had no doubt worked out what a disservice her mother had done her, and that would only add to their already strained relationship.

Ruby had met with the Council several times over the years attempting to get their help in forcing Carla to begin training Kathleen, but they had insisted the Fates would play out as they were intended. *Yeah and didn't that just sound like a bunch of old jack asses sitting all safe and sassy behind their enormous, jewel encrusted table.* The arched table reminded Ruby of a judge's bench because it was elevated and the front was enclosed. She'd always wondered what the members wore for shoes during their long, tedious hours of tending to the business of the magical community. She'd always fancied the belief that they wore something with some pizazz because Lord and Leapers, those robes they wore were butt-ugly as Ruby had heard the younger witches describe them.

One of Ruby's favorite ways to pass the time when she was waiting to speak with the Council was to sit in the long hallway outside their chambers and visit with the younger generation. She'd often learned things of great value during those conversations, and with the increasing pressures to succeed, youngsters were especially vulnerable to the temptations of the dark side of magic. It never ceased to amaze Ruby how easily those without any real experience can be seduced by their own power or with promises of more power.

CHAPTER FOURTEEN

K IT WALKED TO the Michael's suite of rooms and knocked softly on the door. When Nick swung the door open, she could see Braden standing behind him. "Kit, what a wonderful surprise. Come on in. Braden, do you remember Kit?"

"Yes, I know her. She is Carla and Ruby's girl. She is also very powerful witch." Kit stood by, completely in awe at the brilliant young wizard.

"Well, I must say I'm terribly impressed, young man. You are something to behold. The next time I need to remember something, I know just who to come to." The good looking blonde's eyes lit up and his rosy cheeks were practically glowing. "I'm here so you and I can start practicing together a bit. My granny tells me that the better we get at knowing what the other one might do the better chance we have of protecting the people we care about. So what do you say? Are you up for some fun?"

"Oh I have always loved Ruby's games. She always made learning fun when we were traveling. She was always more fun than Carla." He leaned close and whispered, "Carla was kind of a fuddy-duddy." When Kit snorted a laugh, he added, "Ruby taught me that. I love those words."

"I don't doubt for a minute Ruby taught you that exact thing. She is great fun, but don't let Carla hear you say that or we'll all be getting the 'respect your elders' speech. And personally, I've already heard it plenty of times for the both of us." Kit and Braden played a variety of games for the next hour. The games were designed to be played quickly and rely on reflexes and being able to anticipate what your opponent might do. Kit was impressed with his understanding and skill. He was clearly very gifted and if he was already this powerful, Kit was having trouble imagining how much more powerful he would become when he turned sixteen next month and his powers came fully on.

While they had played, Nick had stood along the wall watching silently. His affection for Braden was easy to see. Kit looked at Nick and grinned, "He's amazing, really. He is smart and quick, and he's going to be smoking me in these games in a big hurry if I don't practice." Turning her attention to Braden, she said, "I hear you are recovering at a remarkable speed. You're body seems to have some mighty impressive regenerative powers." And that was going to go down as one of the most absurd understatements of all time. Braden's leg had been shattered in the explosion and Angie had worked hours to piece it back together with a variety hardware, and what should have taken months to heal was almost completely healed in just a couple of weeks. Nick was working with him on physical therapy, and from what Kit had heard, he was almost back to one hundred percent.

Braden smiled, "Angie is pretty amazing. If she hadn't pieced me back together so perfectly, I'd never have healed so completely." When the young man looked at Nick, he asked, "Can we tell her about what Julie said?" The hope in his voice was easy to hear and the softness in Nick's eyes was easy to read as well. Kit didn't have the heart to steal his thunder by telling him that she'd already heard the wonderful news. So when Nick nodded knowingly and winked at her after Braden had returned his gaze to her, Kit simply smiled and listened.

"Julie has been checking…you know, since usually my kind of magic draws more from blood relatives…well, that maybe Angie and I are related. When I was still with my dad he used to talk about family in America, but I don't remember him giving me any names, and I'm usually pretty good at remembering stuff." He blushed and Kit laughed.

"I'm sure that's right. Mercy, I'd love to have your memory."

"Thanks. If it turns out Angie and I have a connection, Julie said that maybe she could manage to get a court order for me to stay here. How cool would that be? I'd have a real home and family again." Kit's heart filled with emotion at the hope in his voice. And even though Kit knew that the Fates were often cruel, she sent up a silent prayer that they would finally shine some kindness on Braden.

Nick must have sensed how close Kit was to an emotional edge because he stepped forward and grinned at Braden. "We're all hoping for that, Braden. Nothing would make the three of us any happier than to have you join our family permanently. And I assure you, we are doing everything we can to locate your maternal grandmother. If there is anyone who can find a spritely professor of chemistry in Ireland, it's Julie Wolf-Edwards."

Kit tilted her head at Nick in curiosity. "What is this? I must not have gotten the latest memo."

Braden's excited voice answered before Nick had even gotten his mouth opened. "I remembered my dad telling me about my mum's mother being some sort of a college professor of chemistry at The University of Dublin. If we can find her, he could give permission for me to stay with Angie, Nick, and Tristan so I'd be safe."

Kit stumbled to her feet in a daze. Was it possible? *There are no coincidences, Kathleen.* Her grandfather's words moved through her mind as if he'd spoken them aloud in the room. But this? This was just too far out of the realm of imagination. Could there be that much alignment in the universe? Kit hadn't even realized Nick was speaking to her until he grasped her arm. "Kit! Are you alright? Do you need me to call your mates?"

"Oh, no. Although they will no doubt be headed this way soon enough. Can I use your phone?" Tapping in Libby's cell number on Nick's phone, she knew the call would go to voice mail because Libby rarely answered her personal phone during mid-terms. She left her friend a brief message asking that she return the call as soon as possible. She had just returned his phone when there was a pounding on the door that caused all three of them to chuckle.

When Jameson and Trev both entered Kit assured them that she was fine, that she had just been blindsided by Braden's comment about his grandmother. And as she'd explained that Libby had spent a couple of semesters at the University of Ireland working with a gifted elderly female professor that she swore was a witch. As she'd been speaking, Braden's skin had started to glisten. When she turned to him in question he grinned. "Sorry, some people get goose bumps and I get…well *this.*"

Kit pulled him into a hug and laughed, "Oh leaping lizards in leotards that is priceless. And believe me, sweet friend, I understand exactly how crazy that is to explain to your friends."

🐾 🐾 🐾

KIT WAS PACING in their suite as her mind whirled. It was unusual for both babies to be asleep at the same time and she was enjoying the chance to sort through questions. She'd been so lost in thought she had only vaguely registered the fact her phone had beeped until her mother strode into the room. *So much for peace and quiet. Give me a crying infant over this any day.* And as if on cue, both babies started wailing from the nursery. Trev was right behind her mom and gave her a shrug of apology and then pointed at the flashing message light on her phone.

"Hello, Mother. What brings you here?" Kit had tried to keep her voice level but filtering out all of the snark was difficult.

"I wanted to check on you after your encounter with Devin. I also wanted to check on Braden and play with the babies." With that, she turned and flounced down the hall toward the nursery.

Trev stepped in front of Kit and pulled her against his chest. Kit knew he could feel the tension rolling off her and she hated being so easily affected by her mother, but there it was. "She isn't staying long, you dad is downstairs speaking with Jameson and he said they were just passing through. He'll be up in a few minutes." Kit felt herself relax at the mention of her dad.

Just at that moment, her mom reemerged from the nursery with a baby propped on each hip. Both Ryan and Adana were eyeing her suspiciously and just as Kit stepped forward, Adana raised her tiny fist and a spark flew from her little fingers and pinged off Carla's earring. "Oh my Lord." Carla's startled cry brought a howl of laughter from behind them, and when Kit turned around her father was trying to bring himself under control.

"Kathleen darling, you did exactly the same thing, although I'm sure you were almost a year old at the time. I'd say our little Adana is gifted indeed." Her dad reached for his granddaughter who leaned toward him immediately. "Come here, darling girl. Now, you be a sweetheart to grandpa, okay?" Kit watched as Adana looked up at her grandfather with eyes filled with adoration. *Oh Lord, talk about an actress! I can practically hear Katherine Hepburn's Oscar record shattering.* Kit smiled as her daughter cuddled her grandpa much to her grandmother's obvious frustration.

Ryan appeared to be more than willing to take up the slack his sister's defection had left in his grandmother's attention. Kit watched her mother smother Ryan with kisses, and being the little ham that he was, her son soaked up the glory like a sponge. Kit looked over at Trev and rolled her eyes causing him to snort out a laugh he quickly tried to play off with a cough.

Kit had managed to chat up her mother for about as long as could be reasonably expected when her phone rang. Seeing Libby's name on the screen, she scooped it up and left the room. The last thing she needed was her mother's involvement with Libby. Libby Wells was a small ball of fire, and even though she didn't have any magical abilities that Kit knew of, she was brilliant and as loyal as they came. "Libby, do you have any pictures of that professor that you worked with in Ireland?"

"Well, hi, Kit. How are you? Oh, my? I'm just jim-friggin' dandy, thanks for asking." Kit could hear the smile in Libby's voice. "Geez, girlfriend, just jump right to it. Yeah, I think so, why? And don't give me any of that loosygoosy answer crap. That ship sailed when I found out about your shifter hubbies and their little group of wilderness hotties. Oh and then there was the little 'my best friend's a witch thing' too. Do you know how many times your magic would have come in handy? Shit, we could have had front seats to every concert and show in the city. You are just lame you know that? Now, why?"

Typical Libby. Full speed ahead. How her mind and mouth could work independently and both at a lightning pace had always fascinated Kit. "The pics are in your inbox, but I still want the deets, so spill."

"Did she ever mention a daughter or grandson?"

"We shared a couple of pints a few times and she mentioned her daughter had died in childbirth, but then she'd get really withdrawn and wouldn't say any more. Hell, I was a visiting doctoral candidate, I didn't want to piss off the head of the department, you know?"

"Holy shit. No actually, I'm not sure I would recognize *that* Libby Wells." Kit had known Libby for several years and had never seen her be anything but straight up and blazingly honest, even when it had not always been the most diplomatic way to handle a situation. "Do you think you could drive out this weekend? I have someone I'd like you to meet."

"You mean you want me to check somebody out and see if they look like Dr. O'Donnell?" Libby's question had been so spot on that Kit was starting to second guess her original observations that Libby wasn't a witch.

"Yeah, something like that. But I don't want to prejudice you. Please?" Kit knew Libby had been spending a lot of time on a big special project for her department that could have broad medical applications. The extra hours meant her friend hadn't been able to take much time off and now Kit was asking her to give up some of it and she felt bad for imposing. "You know I wouldn't ask if it wasn't really important. And I promise to tell you everything. Libby, this concerns the safety of my children or I wouldn't push you."

The silence was deafening, and maybe Kit should have felt bad about playing the baby card when Libby was their Godmother, but sometimes when you are dealing with exhausted, stressed out geniuses you have to pull out the big guns.

"You are a heartless bitch. That was just cold. I don't even know why I like you." Libby took a deep breath and let it out on a sigh. "Okay, but I'm only staying an hour. And I need a ride, my car is in the shop. And whoever the beastie boys send better be hot."

Chapter Fifteen

Two days later, Kit sat on the sofa with Libby and looked at the dark purple circles under her eyes. "Libby, you really need to wrap up this project before you make yourself ill. I'm starting to think you need a couple of Doms in your life to ensure you take better care of yourself." The "benefits" of submission had become something of a running debate between them. Kit was always trying to tell Libby there was more to it than being bossed around, but so far her pint-sized pal was a no-sale.

"Sure that's just what I need, a couple of hotties waving their big cocks at me to convince me sex is better after they beat me for not being home to make their dinner." Libby's words were saying one thing, but her eyes were saying another.

"I think it's safe to assume with cooking skills like ours, they wouldn't be asking you to cook their dinner. But it's a safe bet they would require you to take better care of yourself, and I can see you getting plenty of punishments for not complying with that." Kit let it her words just float between them for a couple of minutes. Before she started to speak again, she carefully considered her words. "You know how we're always hearing that there are no coincidences?"

"Yeah. And I swear the more I'm around you and the chaos that seems to be attracted to you like a magnet, the

105

more I believe it." Kit knew Libby was only partially kidding and something about that hurt her feelings just a little bit. Libby must have noticed and she visibly cringed, "Damn, Kit, I'm sorry. I really didn't mean it like that. It's just that all kinds of interesting things happen to you and I feel like the ugly, boring, nerdy friend who watches from the second or third row." Libby took a deep breath and let it out slowly before continuing. "It's just that I'm thirty, I don't have a social life *at all* since you got married and moved here. I work seventy plus hours a week, and it's not likely I'll ever find someone at this rate." The bleak look in Libby's eyes made Kit's heart clinch in guilt because even though Libby might like to present a professional hard-ass front, she was, at heart, a gentle and loving spirit who thrived on being needed and nurtured.

"I'm so glad you came out today. I needed my Libby-fix and with things the way they are, it isn't safe for me to travel into the city alone. Let me update you on things and then I have a surprise for you." Kit had arranged for them to both get a massage and then they were going to have a very liquid lunch on the terrace. As she explained all the recent happenings and her training, Libby had been transfixed with her eyes as wide as a child's on Christmas morning.

"Holy hat racks and hand stands, Kit. You have the most interesting life of anyone I know. Lord but I wish you lived closer so I could just hang out and live vicariously." Libby's voice was awash with childlike enthusiasm that had her practically bouncing in her seat.

Kit shook her head at Libby's antics, but when she grasped her friend's hand, she gasped. "Oh my God Libby, what the hell?" The depth of Libby's exhaustion washed through Kit so fast that she felt her own energy level dip before she could block it. Pulling herself back up, Kit started funneling energy through their skin-to-skin connection.

She watched Libby's eyes widen in surprise. "Oh my God, Kit. My entire body is tingling, what are you doing?" Kit watched as color slowly filled Libby's pixie face and her cheeks turned a nice healthy pink. Kit didn't completely finish because she'd need to recharge herself first, but she'd made a nice dent in her friend's exhausted state.

Just as she opened her mouth to answer, the room started filling with people, so Kit held back her response. If her husbands knew how generously she'd "shared" her energy with Libby they would *understand,* but they wouldn't be particularly thrilled with the idea. When Braden walked in, Libby's eyes widened.

Ordinarily, Braden had was shy around strangers, but he was also insatiably curious. And since he'd known why Libby was visiting, he made his way straight over to them. To Libby's credit, she didn't even flinch, she simply stood and held out her hand. "Braden, it's nice to meet you. Kit has told me about you and I brought some pictures for you to look at. I know I sent them to Kit, but there is nothing like holding a picture in your hands, is there?"

Braden's eyes had gone from wary to completely enthralled when his palm had connected with Libby's, and Kit had seen Nick and Tristan visibly relax. She'd wished Angie could have been here, but she'd been called in when Libby had already been on her way. Kit knew Braden had "read" her friend in an instant and anything Libby actually said was going to be repetitious at this point but watching closely, she grinned as Braden fell under what Kit had always referred to as the "Libby Effect."

Libby Wells had her own "magic" in that she was able

to spread her joy to almost every person she came in contact with. Kit had often been envious of Libby's ability to "light up a room" with her contagious enthusiasm. Libby quickly pulled Braden next to her as she sat back down and handed him a stack of pictures. Everyone in the room seemed to be holding their breath as the young man they had all come to care so deeply about slowly flipped through the pictures. Libby had patiently explained each print, telling him anecdotes about them. He'd nodded his understanding but hadn't seemed to "recognize" anything until a picture of a small cottage near a cliff caught his attention.

"I've been here. I remember this place. There is a cobblestone walk from a drive that you can't see in this picture. The surf sounds like it's pounding the rocks and the intensity changes with the moon." Kit could see his hands were visibly shaking and his expression was the most animated she'd ever seen on his sweet face. "There is a stairway that leads down to a small beach, but I wasn't allowed to go down there alone. And inside there are only a few rooms, but there is a large room in the basement that is hidden. I had to stay down there one time. It seemed like I was there for days, but it probably wasn't. I was just a little kid, you know?" Everyone watched as he ran his fingers over the print, obviously lost in the memory. Kit knew how hard it was to sort through what was real and what was imagined for magical children. All kids have the same trouble to some extent because their imaginations are so rich and vibrant. But witches had the added struggle of actually *seeing* so much that others would never experience, it was particularly hard to bring it back and sort through it as an adult.

"After that day, we had to start moving all the time,

and I never got to go back there. That day was the first time I'd ever seen my dad shift, and it was cool and scary at the same time." Braden looked up at Libby, and Kit felt her heart clench for him. He'd lost so much in his short life, it just didn't seem fair for a child to be punished because he possessed gifts and abilities he'd never asked for.

Libby looked at him and smiled, "Well, Braden, I can't tell you how pleased I am to tell you that this is what my mentor referred to as her cottage retreat. She took me to visit it once. She said it held very treasured memories of someone she'd loved enough to let go. I'd always assumed she was talking about a man in her life, but I'm pretty sure now she was talking about you."

Braden's entire face lit up as if Libby had just handed him the secrets of the universe. "You mean it's true? That there really is still someone living who would have known my mom? Someone who could tell me about her? Because that would be amazing, you know?"

Suddenly the entire room erupted in a symphony of voices as everyone started sharing their opinions about how to best introduce Braden to his maternal grandmother and keep him safe at the same time. Nick had pulled Braden to his feet and wrapped him in a bear hug before passing him over to Tristan. And during the chaos, Kit reached over to Libby, "Do you think she'll be willing to talk to him? What is she like? Will the memories be too much? Is she going to be willing to put herself at that risk?"

Libby sighed looking over at Kit, "Honestly? I just don't know. She seemed horribly sad the day she took me there. And you have to remember, that was several years ago, and she was *elderly* at that point. I just don't know how she'll react, but I'm willing to try to arrange it if you think it will help."

Tristan stepped forward and shook his head and Kit worried that he was angry. But he knelt in front of her and pulled her hands into his, "Kit, I don't know how you put it all together, but I can't tell you how grateful we are. Finding his grandmother and having the opportunity to speak with her will go a long way in answering his questions." Turning to Libby, he added, "We don't want to put her in any danger, but if she'd be willing to participate in a video conference with Braden, that would be great. Would you speak with her, Libby?"

"Absolutely. The time difference is always a challenge, but if you'll give me a few minutes and a laptop, I'll email her and try to explain what's happened. She'll answer either way, but I just don't know what that answer will be." Tristan helped them both stand then led Libby to his office, and Kit was left standing in the middle of a room full of chattering people but she was suddenly chilled as if her soul was being tossed about in a shifting wind. There was a storm brewing. She could feel the winds of change stirring and the fact that she knew there was an important piece of the puzzle still missing was unsettling.

Chapter Sixteen

Kit's phone sparked to life the next morning long before she was ready to consider the fact it was a new day. Rolling over Jameson's warm chest and reaching for her phone, she gasped out her greeting when her mate slid his hand between the folds of her sex. Libby's laughter on the other end let Kit know her ever intuitive friend hadn't missed it. "I'm not even going to ask. I don't want to know." Laughter was ringing through her words. "Good news, Dr. O'Donnell agreed to Skype with Braden. Honestly, her email sounded kind of excited and beyond relieved to know that he was in a safe place. How is tomorrow afternoon at two? That will make it seven in the evening, and she will be home from her office by then."

They quickly finalized their plans with Jameson and Trev who had actively tuned in when they'd heard Libby's voice coming from her phone. After they'd disconnected, Jameson growled and pulled her over him. "Mate, our run last night was amazing. Sliding my cock into you out under the stars is just about as good as it gets. Seeing you arch your slender back in invitation as you surrender your body to me while lying in lush waves of soft grass is magic on a level that imprints itself on my heart. And watching as you run through the woods with the wind whipping all that lovely rust colored fur is a sight to behold." His erection had found its way between her legs and he was rocking her back and forth so the length was stimulating every inch of the petals of her pussy. Moaning in pure need, she felt her desire rocketing upward. Feeling her juices making the slide smoother with each pass, Kit leaned down and circled his nipple with her tongue. Jameson's growl was so deep in his chest she was sure it was going to rumble for a full minute before managing to make its way up to his throat.

After the disaster in the dungeon, they had talked several times about their individual needs and expectations, and the result had strengthened their connection. Kit felt like the new intensity of their bond was the lifeline she'd been thrown. It had pulled from a swirling sea of uncertainty and she'd thanked Marcus and Reagan for their help.

Kit was quickly losing herself in the deep end of a swirling pool of sensation and she was vaguely aware of Trev moving behind her. Leaning over her, he opened his mouth and bit down gently on the tender spot where her shoulder and neck joined—the same spot where he had bitten when he'd claimed her. His teeth held her firmly for several seconds, but didn't pierce her skin. Releasing her, he licked her ear and then spoke against the wet flesh. "Know what would have made it perfect, baby?"

"What?" Kit's response had been little more than a short gasp.

A stinging swat landed on her bare ass, and she groaned. The pain raced straight to her clit and screamed "pleasure ahead" at a volume that was impossible to ignore. It had taken several seconds of them holding perfectly still before Kit realized her mistake. "What would have made it perfect, Sir?"

"Oh that was so much better, baby." Trev's voice was filled with seduction and the tone that Kit had always thought of as his "happy Dom" voice. "The only thing better than us fucking you individually in the moonlight is fucking you together in the moonlight. And if you'll notice there is still a tiny bit of that streaming in through the window since Libby evidently has no qualms about calling at three a.m." There was a slight lilt of amusement running through the last of his words, but Kit's body was busy appreciating the feel of his fingers massaging lube in and around her rear hole to really put everything together.

The feel of his fingers pressing against her most sensitive hole shot her lust into the stratosphere and by the time he'd added a second finger, she was arching and trying to press back for more. Jameson's arm banded tightly around her, stilling her movements before just before they reached fever pitch. "Hold still, mate. Let Trev prepare you properly, you are ours to protect even when you don't want to be patient." Kit knew his words held more meaning than just this moment, but right now that was all her mind could wrap itself around. Every single cell in her body felt like it was reeling because she'd gone from speaking with Libby to fully aroused in mere seconds. *Yes! These are the men I fell in love with. I knew they were in there somewhere.*

"Oh yes, kitten, we are indeed right here and right here we plan to stay. We'll always be right beside you, sweetheart, all you need to do is reach out your hand and take what is yours...just as we are planning to take what is ours." Just as Jameson spoke those words, she felt Trev press the end of his cock against her ass. The heat of his cockhead warmed her pucker and it relaxed against the invasion.

"Fuck me, she is so hot and tight. That's a good girl, keep pushing out. Christ, mate, your body is fucking perfect." Kit was losing herself in the moment but felt satisfaction move through her knowing she'd put that desperation in her mate's voice. Once Trev was nearly all the way in, Jameson unwrapped his arms and let Trev lift her just enough that he could push into her sheath. Kit placed her hands on Jameson's broad chest and flexed her fingers enough to lightly score his skin. His growl sent a spear of white hot pleasure through her and she saw her skin begin to shimmer as her orgasm approached. Kit felt her mates begin alternating their long, slow strokes, and having one of them inside her at all times, kept the stimulation at a level that made rational thought all but impossible.

"Please," was all she managed before her entire body began tingling.

"Holy shit that's hot. Her entire body is literally vibrating. Come for us, mate." Jameson's voice was passion-filled and Kit's mind appreciated the fact she'd been able to bring him to that point, but she'd lost any ability to respond as wave after wave of pleasure crashed through her body. Every one of her senses was on overload and the scream that rent the air was brief before Jameson sealed his mouth over hers and absorbed the sound.

Their pace had slowed as she started to return to earth and realized they hadn't come yet. The instant the realization floated through her endorphin saturated mind, both men began relentlessly pushing in and pulling out in a carefully choreographed rhythm that reignited her pleasure before the embers of her last fire had a chance to cool. As their pace picked up so did the pulsing energy surrounding them, and Kit's magic fed off that response. Every candle in the room suddenly glowed bright, and in the back of her mind she registered their satisfaction. The shimmering that had dimmed after her first orgasm had flared back even more vividly, and the flickering light actually began to emit waves of fluorescent colors. As both men sunk in balls deep and shouted her name, she felt the pulses of their seed inside her body and that sensation alone was enough to send her careening into another soaring release. Lights danced behind her eyelids, and then she suddenly felt as if she were floating in space because everything was blissfully quiet and a deep sense of peace descended over her and wrapped itself around her mind like a warm blanket.

JAMESON FELT COMPLETELY leveled by the magnitude of the release his body had just experienced. Holding Kit against him, he knew instinctively that she had passed out and he wondered how the hell Trev was managing to avoid collapsing atop them both.

I'll move in a minute or thirty. Christ Almighty, I don't have any feeling in my legs yet. I'm just barely managing to not fall on top of our mate. Jameson was actually grateful that he wasn't in Trev's position because he wasn't sure his arms would have held him up. There had been an unmistakable intensity to each sexual encounter they'd had with Kit since the day she had safe worded out in the dungeon that Jameson had noticed but wasn't sure he could explain. It was if they had all realized how close they'd come to letting their greatest possession slip through their fingers. He and Trev had spoken with Kit together and individually, and he was sure those conversations had made all the difference. He was grateful for Marcus and Reagan's wisdom and guidance, but at the end of the day it had been the deep love the three of them shared that had seen them through. And now, with everything coming together for

Braden, the joy of family was even more apparent.

When he felt Trev finally move from the bed, Jameson gently rolled Kit to the side and held her against his chest, wrapped safely in his arms. Remarkably, she seemed to have slipped into a deep sleep. After they'd cleaned her up and dried her tender tissues, Trev returned to bed and took her into his arms. Jameson staggered into the shower and let the hot water massage the tension from his shoulders. Losing himself in his plans for the day, he started laying out all the things that needed to be done and brought himself up short. Shaking his head, he realized how easily he'd slipped back into the role of a single Alpha. He knew he needed to start delegating more duties to those he claimed to trust. Remembering that his fathers had cautioned Trev and him against micromanaging the pack. "Don't ever forget your duties to your mate or your pack. And remember they are equally important." His dad's words sounded through his mind as if he was standing right next to him.

Changing his plans, he decided to let Tristan and Nick manage the Skype call, and he hoped that Angie would be able to be present. He'd been considering offering her a full-time position in their clinic, but he wasn't sure she was ready to entertain that change just yet. She was a gifted researcher and perhaps a state of the art lab would sweeten the deal. Even he could see his driven cousin was about to push herself beyond her limits, and he knew her mates were nearing the point their patience had finally been drained. Jameson worried the flash fire of his friends' tempers would leave behind nothing but ashes.

Jameson considered his fathers continually emphasizing to both he and Trev that a large part of being an effective Alpha was knowing when people needed your help and when they needed to struggle in order to learn a life lesson. He'd let Angie struggle, but he felt like the time had come where he needed to make sure she was once again set on the right path. Angie's behavior was typical "Angie"...stubborn. And the more her mates pushed the harder she had been pushing back. Reaching out of the shower, he grabbed his phone and typed in a quick text to her. He smiled when he got an immediate response telling him the meeting time he'd given her wasn't "convenient" for her. His "make it convenient" response hadn't earned him a response, but he knew she'd be in his office at the scheduled time. There were a lot of disadvantages to being the pack Alpha, but there were certainly some great perks as well. And being able to demand a pack member's compliance when it was deemed necessary was certainly one of the best perks he'd found.

As soon as he'd dressed, he made his way down to his office to begin his day. Jameson had always loved this quiet time. He'd learned early on that he was usually able to get through a great deal of the day's business before the rest of the mansion came to life. He was just getting ready to go in search of coffee when Ruby came through the door carrying a small tray with three mugs of steaming coffee and breakfast cakes. "Good morning, Jameson, I believe you were ready for this?" All he could do was shake his head and chuckle.

"You already know that I was. Who will be joining us?" He really was fond of the older witch and she was quickly spoiling him rotten.

"Trev will be here in a minute, but I wanted to thank you for everything you have done for Braden. I realize that having him here is a risk to every member of your pack. And your willingness to provide him a safe port in the storm has not gone unnoticed by The Supreme Council."

Jameson wasn't sure why that should matter to him so he merely nodded his head letting the saucy little woman know he'd heard her. "I understand that you might not fully understand the importance of their support, but I assure you it will become more apparent in the future. Building bridges is always better than burning them, if you understand my meaning." She winked at him over the top edge of the mug she was sipping from. Her eyes were sparkling with mischief and he wondered for just a moment what it took for a person to remain that upbeat after all the pain and suffering she'd been witness to.

Jameson did indeed understand that part of her message. It had always been his experience that building alliances—without fail, paid off down the road, and usually in ways he could have never imagined at the time he'd "paid it forward." He chose his words carefully, "That I do understand, Ruby. And I assure you we'll always help anyone when we can. Our dads instilled in us a strong sense of right and wrong. And one of the things they taught was that the measure of a man was how many people he'd helped during his life because that was the real legacy he'd leave behind."

Ruby's eyes filled with unshed tears for just a moment and then she smiled. "I remember both of your fathers as well as your lovely mother. They were wonderful people and they taught you and Trevlon well. I'm sure they watch you from the other side of the veil and are very proud of the leaders you have become." She took another lingering sip of the steaming coffee in her colorful mug before continuing. "And I used the word leader purposely. Being the Alpha of a pack is merely a title, but being a leader is a description...don't ever forget there is a difference."

Trev walked in and spied the coffee on the tray and

quickly made his way over. Kissing Ruby on the cheek, he winked, "You are a blessing in many ways, Granny Good Witch, but this has to be right up there close to the top." Jameson watched as her cheeks blushed and he couldn't hold back his laughter.

Once they'd all settled in the sitting area of Jameson and Trev's office, Ruby looked up and sighed. "I have just returned from a meeting with the Council and they've sent me to warn you of a coming confrontation. Devin has been recruiting support among those who have dark side ambitions, and it appears he's gathered a significant number of followers. The Council has detained several applicants for intern positions who have connections to Devin." She seemed lost in thought for several seconds as she sat mutely staring out the window as the coral colored streaks of dawn painted the sky.

Ruby finally seemed to refocus on the conversation and continued. "They have four targets: Kit, Ryan, Adana, and Braden. We can shield the entire estate, but each time a pack member travels in or out they weaken the effectiveness of the protection the shield provides. So the first thing we're requesting is that you limit the traffic as much as you can."

Jameson's mind was immediately set on fast forward as he mentally reviewed which pack members traveled outside the compound each day to work. Julie Wolf-Edwards and her husband, Lance, had a loft in the city and he was sure they'd choose to stay there since neither had skills that would be particularly helpful during a magical showdown. Julie was a shifter, but her mate wasn't. Lance Edwards was a well-known actor, and even though his acting skills made him obscene amounts of money, they wouldn't be much help in this instance. And the truth was, the fewer people they had to worry about and protect, the easier things would be for his security team and the witches who would be working to keep everyone safe.

Jameson used his mind link to send word out to Tristan and Nick to schedule the Skype and also gather the rest of the security team for a meeting as quickly as possible. Turning to Ruby, he asked, "Will you stay and meet with our security people? I'd like them to hear as much of the information as possible directly from you. There is less chance for details to be lost and they'll ask questions that I'm sure you can answer better than either Trev or I can." She hadn't hesitated in her agreement, and Jameson once again found himself being amazed at the older woman's energy because it was obvious she was pushing against the exhaustion he knew followed magical travel. *I hope like hell I'm just as energetic, fun, and quick-witted at her age.*

Ruby's eyes had softened and she moved to him and wrapped her arms around his waist. She gave him a long hug before she told them she was headed up to see the babies. "You'll be a wonderful father and grandfather, Jameson. Just remember that there is more to life than work. You have to find joy in every single day, that's the key." She strolled from the room, and Jameson smiled as she closed the door behind her.

Trev's voice brought him back to the moment, "She is incredible. And Kit swears that she seems to have taken on a lot of her grandfather's characteristics since he passed, which is interesting. I wonder about that at times...Kit and I were talking when we walked through the gardens the other night, do you suppose that the souls of those we've lost can integrate themselves into those who are still here if they have unfinished business?"

Jameson stared at him blankly for several seconds trying to wrap his mind around the concept. "Do you mean like a possession?"

Trev shook his head as if clearing his thoughts, "Not really *possession*, more like a *merging*. I don't know. We were just brainstorming and it made me wonder. How many times have we commented that something we did or said was out of character for us, but sounded exactly like something one of our dads might have done?" Trev sighed softly and then chuckled, "Never mind, that is a question for another day."

CHAPTER SEVENTEEN

KIT WATCHED BRADEN pace back and forth in front of the windows of the office and she could literally see the tension shimmering around him. If she didn't get him calmed down before the Skype call with his grandmother, he wasn't going to be in the right place emotionally to enjoy it. And she doubted he'd even remember the call he'd been looking forward to so much if he wasn't settled by then. "Braden, let's play a game. I'll visualize an object and I want you to conjure it as quickly as you can. We'll start with easier objects and work our way up. For every one you get correct, I'll up your birthday gift by ten percent."

He turned and smiled, looking every bit the teenager he was. "You are getting me a birthday gift?"

"Oh course. You are a member of our pack now. And besides, you are practically family. And you know what? Since I like you...I won't cook." She giggled and then leaned closer to whisper, "Angie is planning a big party, but don't you dare tell her I told you. I just didn't want to deprive you of the anticipation, because for me that is always half the fun." He'd nodded his head and his grin had spread over his entire face. He really was a great kid, and she sent up a silent plea to the Fates that this call would be a blessing rather than a curse for a youngster who had already lost so much. "Okay. Let's start." Kit quickly visualized a brightly colored beach ball and within seconds one appeared at her feet. "Holy crap, buddy. I didn't even see you move."

"Umm, Ruby told me that if I didn't have to use my hands, I shouldn't. That it would help me in the battles because I might be restrained and just using my mind would be helpful." The hesitance and concern in his voice caused Kit to quickly look up. "Is that okay?"

"Are you kidding? It's amazing and I'm totally envious. Good God Gertie, I'm going to have to really start practicing, you're going to smoke my ass." She laughed and saw the relief in his eyes when he joined in her laughter. "Okay, again." Visualizing a floating ball of fire, she wasn't surprised this time when one appeared to be floating right in front of her. Using her mind, she started slowly moving it from side to side. She could feel his mind link to hers as he tried to help and direct her focus. In just a few minutes they were batting the ball of fire back and forth between them in a slow motion version of tennis that quickly had her breaking a sweat just from the effort to keep up with him.

When the door opened the ball immediately evaporated. When Kit looked up she didn't recognize the man standing in the doorway smiling at them. "I must say, that was very impressive considering Braden's youth and the fact that you've only been training for a short time, Kathleen. Yes, mighty impressive indeed." He'd continued walking until he was standing in front of them, and Kit fought the urge to step in front of Braden and shield him from the new comer. He must have sensed her trepidation because he chuckled. "Aww, those protective mothering instincts are very powerful, aren't they, dear? Well I assure you, neither of you has anything to fear from me."

By this time her grandmother had moved so she was standing next to the stranger who surprisingly seemed to look an awful lot like Professor Dumbledore in the Harry Potter movies. He shook his head and grinned as he leaned forward and whispered, "That wasn't one of my smarter moves, you know. Planting that seed in the mind of the director was pure ego on my part. Who knew every kid and most of the adults in the world were going to see those movies? But the Fates have gotten the last laugh I assure you, because now everyone thinks I look like the good Professor rather than the other way around."

Ruby laughed out loud and then said, "Cecil, we tried to tell you. But you were so sure it would be the best joke ever." *Cecil? What kind of wizard is named Cecil? Good grief.*

"You see, Ruby—that is exactly why I did it. Nobody takes a wizard named Cecil seriously." The old man's face was heavily lined and the lines deepened when he smiled. His white beard reached the top of his chest and his small, round spectacles highlighted beautiful brown eyes. He wasn't particularly tall, but he was probably close to six foot with a slender build. Kit bet the distinguished looking gentleman standing before her had been absolutely dashing as a younger man. And he appeared to have a great sense of humor, which had put everyone in the room at ease right away. His suit was a dark navy and his white shirt was open at the collar, helping him seem less formal, which was an added benefit when dealing with a teenager. He leaned forward and extended his hand to Braden first, "Hello, Braden. It's nice to finally meet you face-to-face. My name is Cecil and I'm a member of the Supreme Council. I'm here to help in any way I can." After he'd shaken Braden's hand, he turned his attention to Kit and repeated the gesture. "I know you have a call to make, so I'm going to leave you to it." Flashing them a grin that hinted at the ornery nature that was lurking just beneath the surface, he added, "I stuck my head in the kitchen before coming in and the cooks were just getting ready to take an apple strudel out of the oven, so I'm off to sample what smelled like heaven on earth. We'll talk after your call." He'd almost made it to the door before turning back to them. "And, Braden, remember your grandmother is an amazing woman. She made an unbelievable sacrifice to keep you safe...remember an attitude of gratitude is often a man's greatest strength."

KIT WATCHED AS Braden was reunited with his maternal grandmother and even though she knew he still had hundreds of questions about his mother, they had to end his portion of the call so Julie could speak with the elderly woman about granting guardianship to the Michaels family. After speaking with Tristan, Nick, and Angie, Serena O'Donnell had agreed to give them guardianship as long as she had unlimited visitation rights. Everyone had agreed it was in Braden's best interest to spend time with her anytime it could be safely arranged.

Dr. O'Donnell had explained to Braden how his mom had died during childbirth and even some of the details of the battle that had sent him and his dad on the run. But Kit had noticed that she had very tactfully avoided questions about his grandfather. She made a mental note to ask Granny Good Witch about that little detail later. Just as the meeting was breaking up and the call had been disconnected, Kit had been distracted by Angie's excitement about becoming Braden's legal guardians. Her friend had barely let Braden out of her reach, and he'd been more than happy to soak up all of the maternal attention.

Making her way over to Braden, she held her hand up for high five and he slapped her hand with enthusiasm and then hugged her close. "Thanks, Kit. I know that you were the one who put the clues together and gave me the chance to meet my grandmother." She could tell his voice had been close to breaking and she just squeezed him tightly and gave him a minute to recover. "I just want you to know that I'll practice every day so I'm ready when the time comes. And I'll protect you and your babies with everything in me...I promise."

Kit couldn't hold back her tears. His words had touched her in a way no one ever had, his gratitude was so genuine, and his promise so sincere, that she felt their souls bond. There was a small part of her that realized this bonding would go a long way to help them coordinate their efforts in a battle, but at this moment, it just felt touching and special. When he pulled back his eyes were still glassy, but his infectious grin had returned. "We did great with the little ball of fire, didn't we? I can't wait to practice outside with some targets. Maybe tomorrow after I finish my lessons and physical therapy?" She nodded and he too headed off toward the kitchen.

Angie stepped into her view and grinned. "You know he is one of the nicest kids I've ever met. And when you consider everything he's been through, his attitude and outlook are amazing. I don't know how to thank your mom for bringing him into our lives."

Kit waved her hands frantically, "Angie...don't say that...it's like tempting Fate or something. You mention her...and she—" that was all Kit got out before her mother swept into the room.

"Did we miss the call? I tried to tell Richard we were going to be late, but do you think he would hurry? Hex me, he is annoying and slower than molasses during a Vermont winter. It was almost as if he was trying to make me late." Kit glanced up at her father who was leaning casually against the doorframe. When their eyes met, her dad winked at her and Kit barely managed to hold back her laughter. He waved his phone at her and glanced at Jameson who winked at her also. Knowing that they had worked together to keep her meddling mother from interfering in Braden's big moment warmed her heart and she blew them both kisses.

"Carla, you did not need to be here for the call. I tried to tell you that on the phone. Braden needed this time without anyone's interference." Ruby Stone's voice had an edge to it that Kit didn't hear often, and she had to suppress the shiver that went through her.

"Interference? Really, mother? You're going to play that card? Honestly, sometimes I think you are becoming senile." *Holy shit, Sherlock, this is going to be a thrown down of biblical proportions if it isn't shut down in a hurry.*

'Watch your language, kitten. And we're monitoring the situation.' Kit mentally rolled her eyes. Sure they were they were the pack Alphas, but these were two very powerful witches, and trying to step into a pissing contest between them would be dim at the minimum and probably extremely dangerous. Deciding that there were times people just needed to learn lessons on their own, Kit just subtly backed up by her dad and settled in to watch the show.

RUBY WAS JUST pissed off, there was no other way to say it.

There was no doubt that her daughter was a powerful witch, but she was also a self-centered bitch who had forgotten what it was like to let the people around her be self-determining. She had let her power go to her head and had forgotten long ago how to be gracious. For the most part, everybody just let her do as she pleased because it was the path of least resistance and much easier than listening to her incessant complaining. But this time Ruby was just at her wit's end with Carla's bratty behavior and she wondered for about the millionth time how on earth her even-tempered son-in-law dealt with her.

Leaning forward just enough to bring Carla's full attention to her, Ruby snarled, "Enough. You are not going to make this all about *you*, because quite frankly, it rarely is. You were late on purpose and by design because that is what I requested. Cecil is in the kitchen as we speak so if you have an issue with how I've handled things today, then by all means feel free to take it up with him." Ruby knew full well that Carla wouldn't make that mistake. It was no secret that the members of the Supreme Council were sharply divided about how to deal with Carla Harris. She was a gifted witch and could easily be promoted to Sorceress if only her attitude was in line with her gifts.

Ruby watched as fire danced in her daughter's expression before she pulled her emotions back under control. Carla turned and smiled at Jameson, "Well, since it seems we've missed this evening's main event, I believe I'll head up and play with the children a bit if that is alright with you." At Jameson's nod, Carla walked regally from the room.

As soon as the door closed behind her parents, Kit started giggling and before long, Ruby had succumbed as well and then they were both laughing hysterically. She knew both Jameson and Trevlon were watching them with a puzzled expression, probably questioning their sanity. In truth, it was a reasonable question, but Ruby just couldn't seem to make herself care.

Chapter Eighteen

S TEPPING OUT THE back door of the mansion, Kit felt the cool redwood planks under her feet and a surge of energy slide up through the soles of her feet. Standing in the moonlight, Kit stretched her arms above her head and felt a shiver of anticipation race through her. The anticipation of a moonlit run in her wolf always sent a rush of adrenaline racing through her, and as Kit looked out over the back meadow, her senses were already intensifying and kicking into high gear. Feeling her skin tingle as her wolf began pressing to the surface, she was glad she had left her sandals inside. Reaching up to stretch out the muscles that had tightened up during dinner with her mother, she sighed as strong arms encircled her from behind. "You weren't going to shift and start without us, were you, baby?" Trev's voice had the low, gravelly tone that was pure promise and erotic seduction wrapped up in one sweet package. His touch alone was enough to send moisture rushing toward her sex in anticipation. His tongue licked up the side of her neck in a slow, moist trail. "I can smell your arousal and if we're actually going to shift and run before I fuck you senseless, we'd better get to it."

Kit felt his hands push under the soft sweatshirt she'd worn and the calloused tips of his fingers were just rough enough to light up the sensitive skin under her breasts. Kit's back arched pressing her nipples against the fabric before his fingertips feathered over the tight peaks. Instinct began to take over and she felt her whole body responding in a cacophony of mixed signals that was quickly pulling her under his spell. Seeking more of his touch, her body and mind were definitely operating on different levels. She wanted to run, hell, she *needed* to run. The tension in the mansion had been almost oppressive the past few days and running under the stars would go a long way toward relieving her stress. But her body's desire to submit to her mate was quickly shoving logic aside.

Moaning as his fingers closed over her tightly drawn nipples, he pulled and rolled them between his thumb and forefinger in varying degrees of pressure. The inconsistency was keeping her enough off balance to assure him she wouldn't come before he was ready for her to. And while she craved his Dominance over her, she still growled in frustration. She felt herself sliding down that steep slope into the place where she easily lost herself in the sensations he was bombarding her with and her empty pussy clenched in anticipation of being filled with her mate's cock. She could feel his hard length pressing against her lower back and wiggled her ass left and right as she pressed back against him in a move that was a part of the mating dance as old as time itself. Her moans were coming on panted breath as her breathing became more and more shallow and she could feel her heart pounding in her chest.

"Your sweet body prepares itself for me in the sweetest ways, baby. I can hear the blood rushing through your veins, and knowing your honeyed pussy is swelling and flowering open like a rose meeting the morning sun is sweet torture because I can feel how badly you need this run." Peeling her shirt over her head in a smooth, practiced move, his hands shackled her wrists over her head. The move was one of pure dominance and it ramped her need for his touch right off the chart.

Kit had been so lost in Trev's seduction that she hadn't realized Jameson had stepped in front of her until his mouth closed over her left nipple. "Oh God, it feels so perfect and I want you both so much I can barely think." Both of her mates growled deep in their throats and she could feel a cracking in the air around them that let her know they were communicating with each other but blocking it from her. Ordinarily she found that habit beyond annoying, but right now there was no question they were planning for her pleasure and she felt her body slipping even further under their influence.

The entire pack had spent the evening celebrating Braden's birthday and would be joining them for tonight's run. Turning sixteen was a major milestone in the life of most young men, but male shifters were able to change when they reached puberty, so tonight wasn't about that for Braden. No, tonight was a celebration of the fact his magical abilities would only be fully manifested at the precise moment he turned sixteen in a couple of hours. Tristan and Nick had only agreed to let him run with the pack tonight after being assured by Cecil that there would be no adverse effects for him if he was in his wolf when the clock struck midnight.

Kit had spent the afternoon with the young man practicing and she knew he was wired for sound about tonight's run. And then she had watched as he had pushed his dinner around on his plate in a useless attempt to convince Angie he was actually eating all the high protein foods she'd piled on his plate. He'd even turned down cake and ice cream, and that had caused the pediatrician in Angie to surface full-force. Kit had shaken her head when Angie had taken his temperature right there in front of everyone. To his credit, Braden had been a good sport and had admitted that turning down either of the special treats certainly wasn't *usual* for him.

"I'm sorry, Sir. But if I don't change soon, we're going to be in a very compromised position when tonight's guest of honor walks out on this deck. And even though he is considered an adult by the magical community at the ripe old age of sixteen, I'm not sure my mind is quite ready for him to see me naked and riding your cock as my other Master slides balls deep into my ass." Kit knew her words were crude, but she knew they'd had their desired effect when both men went completely still for several seconds before erupting into action.

Jameson slid her yoga pants down and moaned when he saw she wasn't wearing panties. He leaned forward and nuzzled her waxed mound and flicked his tongue over her clit causing it to push further from under its hood seeking his attention. Running his tongue slowly through her dripping folds, he lapped at her...reminding her she wasn't the only one barely restraining her wolf. Her legs parted on their own volition giving him more access and she was trembling in mere seconds, so close to climax that she felt her inner walls begin to flutter.

Trev's hands grasped her shoulders and turned her into his arms and Kit felt her heart kick into a full gallop when she realized he'd stripped and was now standing before her gloriously nude and fully aroused. Running her hands over his broad chest, feeling all the dips and ridges of his well-toned body, might not have been the biggest help to maintaining her control, but it was doing wonders for her soul's aching desire for her mates. "I want you, Sir. I want to feel your body sliding against mine as you take ownership of my pleasure."

"Fuck me." The strain in his voice let her know he was as close to the edge of control as she was. "Come on, let's go. The others are already on their way and we are a split second from giving a live porno show to everyone who walks out onto this deck tonight. Kit knew Jameson was already nude because she could hear the popping and cracking of bones changing as he shifted behind her. Trev's hands left her and she launched herself off the deck and was fully shifted before she'd landed in the soft dew-kissed grass. They had discovered early on that she was actually able to shift faster and had attributed it to the fact that she was a witch. She didn't really care *why* it was true, she just used the skill shamelessly as she dug in and took off in a dead run as soon as the pads of her feet connected with the soft grass.

The feeling of the cool, crisp night air ruffling her fur made her push herself to run even faster. The tingling tickles as her body came to full sensual awareness told her that her mates were closing in on her quickly. She might be able to shift faster, but their larger sizes and greater muscular strength always allowed them to catch up quickly. Kit enjoyed the run and the easy rhythm they found together as they explored the trails through the woods surrounding the pack's large estate. When they entered a small but secluded meadow, Jameson reached over and nipped her shoulder. Kit knew exactly what he was demanding and she was more than happy to comply.

Stopping in the small clearing, the three of them circled the small opening in the trees to be sure they were alone before giving in to nature's demands and their own soul's deep need to mate. Those feelings had been pushing them all ever since the foreplay on the back deck, and there was no pushing them back now. They didn't always mate in their wolf form because wolves were notoriously distracted during mating so it was often dangerous. Male wolves totally focus on possessing their mate so they are often not aware of threats to their safety until it is too late. Anything that leaves them that vulnerable was a concern. Lowering the front half of her body and presenting her sex to her mates was almost as satisfying as the act itself…*almost.*

Feeling Jameson's tongue move over the sensitive tissues, checking her readiness, sent a shiver of pure desire racing up Kit's spine. *'Oh that feels so incredible. It lights up every part of me and makes me lose focus on everything but getting you inside me as quickly as possible.'*

'Kitten, nothing short of the apocalypse is going to keep me from sliding my cock inside your sweet body.' When she felt him poised at her entrance and heard his growl, she let herself fall into the submissive state that let her mind prepare itself for the trip into oblivion she knew was coming.

'Baby, the only thing better than fucking you is watching my brother take you. Feel how much he wants you? His desire is only matched by my own. Feeling your wet heat as we push into your waiting warmth is as close to heaven as we'll ever find on earth.' Kit knew Trev had taken over the communication because Jameson was totally distracted as he pumped his hard length in and out of her dripping pussy. He'd been holding her firmly with his teeth clamped over her mating mark and just before he exploded inside her, she felt him tighten the hold just enough to puncture the skin and the sting was exactly the push she'd needed to send her careening over the edge into pure bliss. Lights flashed behind her closed lids and she marveled at how similar an orgasm in her wolf was to that as a human. Evidently, endorphins worked the

same no matter which brain they were bathing in pleasure. After withdrawing from her body, Jameson licked her tender outer lips and cleaned her sex tenderly before howling his claiming for all his pack to hear.

Trev moved in behind her and licked her for long minutes letting her body settle before he began pushing her toward the summit again. *'You smell so sweetly fucked, baby. I can hardly wait to send you right back to heaven. I want you to envision a snowball being pushed down a mountain. Your body is going to gain speed and swell with desire as I take you, and at the bottom of that steep slope is a large boulder that is going to explode that beautiful snow into a million pieces. That is how your release is going to feel...like an explosion of pure white...crisp and clean.'* Kit wasn't sure her release was going to hold off long enough for that damned snowball to get to the bottom if he kept talking to her like that.

He curled his tongue into a still roll and fucked it in and out of her for several seconds and her body ramped back up so quickly she was panting and shaking so hard she wasn't sure her hind legs were going to hold her up. *'Please, Sir. I need you inside me...NOW!'* She heard his chuckle drift through her lust-laden mind just before he slammed into her with enough force to push her nose into the soft grass. He body launched into a frantic pace as she envisioned the snowball he'd mentioned. The visual was a powerful one and as he fucked her with barely restrained strength, she saw that ball of snow grow in her mind until it collided with the boulder just as he'd described and disintegrated. Her entire body clenched as she screamed his name in her mind over and over. Each of the hot jets of his seed pumping in to her sheath pushed her further and further into oblivion. She wasn't sure how long their mutual release lasted, but it was the most drawn out orgasm she had ever experienced.

Collapsing under Trev's weight, Kit could feel her muscles quivering from the exertion of being tensed for so long. All those happy dancing little endorphins flooding her mind were making her almost giddy and she might have actually danced for joy right along with them if she had been able to make her body cooperate. Trev's voice finally penetrated the fog she'd been floating in. *'Baby, I think you just stole my soul. Fucking hell, you have owned me since the moment we met, but this? This was just so far beyond description I can't even begin to sort it out.'* Kit's heart swelled at Trev's words and she was overwhelmed by the depth of her feelings for them.

Chapter Nineteen

JAMESON AND TREV had prodded her awake with their muzzles nuzzling her neck and tiny nips around her ears. *'Come on, baby, time to rise and shine before we lose the best of the moonlight.'* Kit was shocked that she'd actually fallen asleep after their intense mating, and wondered how long she'd slept. *'Don't worry, we didn't let you sleep long. There is a strange energy moving through the forest and we want to get you home. We're going to take a short cut and several of our pack members will be meeting us just up ahead.'*

They'd begun running again once she finally managed to get her legs to follow her mind's instructions. Kit had always thought the erotic romances she'd read had merely been overly dramatic when they'd spoken about the power of an orgasm to completely level you...*but evidently it was true.* For just a moment she considered how grateful she was that Jameson and Trev had been able to stand watch while she'd loved them because she wouldn't have heard an Abrams Tank approach. They always considered her safety above all else during their runs and she hoped they knew how much that meant to her.

'Kitten, when we emerge from this stand of trees there is a large ravine about thirty yards ahead. I want you to veer left as soon as you can so we don't run too close to the ledge.' Jameson's words pushed into her mind and that was when she realized they were in a section of the estate she'd never

seen before. Obviously she'd run a lot further from the mansion that she had realized. She hadn't meant to push so hard, but clearly the stress of the past few days had finally caught up with her. Kit knew they had let her take the lead, obviously sensing her need to run off some steam. But she'd always enjoyed the security of knowing both Jameson and Trev were right behind her and she had been able to simply lose herself in the joy of running.

When they'd begun running again, the moon's light had been softened as clouds began drifting overhead in lazy patches. They looked like loosely woven gauzy curtains drifting in a cool summer breeze, and Kit wondered at the odd chill she felt rippling through the air. Her mates were right, there was a peculiar energy lingering about, and the fact she wasn't able to identify it worried her.

Just as she cleared the trees, the moon emerged again and the intensity of the light had her slowing her pace and looking over the grassy ledge. One of the things Kit relished about being in her wolf was her enhanced night vision. And once the moon's light had returned to its earlier brilliance, the light kissed everything making the whole area almost glow with a luminescence that was almost mystical. *It is incredibly beautiful here.* Kit had already stopped and was standing close to the edge of the ravine by the time her mates moved along her left side. The earth shook slightly beneath her feet and every one of Kit's senses kicked into his gear. When she looked to her right she saw a large gray wolf approaching. His eyes glowed with affection and she recognized Braden's spirit an instant before she saw Tristan, Nick, and Angie.

'Did you feel the earth shake?' Braden's ability to speak to her so clearly surprised her although she wasn't sure why.

'Yes, but I don't know what it was. But I do know it was

close.'

'It happened precisely at midnight.' Kit didn't get a chance to ask him how he knew the time because a pillar of gray smoke rose from the depths of the ravine distracting them both. Sensing the danger, she shifted back into her human form and with barely a nod, was completely clothed. In her peripheral vision, Kit saw that Braden had done the same and they assumed the angled shoulder-to-shoulder position they'd rehearsed so often. Their stance allowed them to see in almost a three hundred and sixty degree arc. Her grandmother and Cecil had both insisted that they work from this position in order to minimize their blind spots, and Kit was suddenly very grateful for their foresight.

The smoke seemed to stall for just a moment before moving forward forcing them to step back several yards. When Kit saw Devin's image begin to appear, she raised her hand in preparation. Standing before them, was Devin in the flowing black robe, and the first thing Kit noticed was the shimmering demon's fork symbol of the dark side's forces gleaming in blood red on his chest. Devin's eyes swept over her and then flicked quickly to Braden. His fleeting glances at the wolves flanking them told Kit just how inconsequential he considered the shifters—a dismissal neither Alpha was taking very well judging by their growls. In truth, they weren't really a threat to him because all he had to do to escape them was vanish back into the mist he'd emerged from.

Kit and Braden had rehearsed their positions many times, but they hadn't ever assumed they'd have one enemy, so it seemed odd to have their bodies angled outward so they shifted slightly so they could both see Devin clearly. Their combined magic would be considerable, and if Devin was spoiling for a fight, they could easily give him one. But for some reason Kit didn't think that was what this little meet and greet was about. She actually had the impression that Devin wasn't all that pleased to see them and that he'd actually been a bit surprised to find them all so close. Deciding she would rather play offense than defense, Kit took the lead. "What do you want, Devin? And why are you on the Wolf Pack's estate?"

There was something different about Devin this time, and Kit wasn't entirely sure what it was. There was a hesitance surrounding him, and that was far different from what she'd encountered before. "I've come to escort Braden to speak with my brother. Damian wants to talk to the boy, that's all." Kit didn't believe that and neither did Devin, if she was reading him correctly. Why he would even make the request was what baffled her. The only possible explanation was that he was being pressured by Damian.

Surprising her, Braden's voice pushed into her mind, *'He doesn't want to do this. Why?'*

'I don't know, but I agree with you. There is a reluctance that I haven't seen before but I'd sure like to know what we're dealing with.' Turning her attention back to the dark haired man standing before her, Kit tried to assess him impartially. He was the epitome of the stereotypical tall, dark, and handsome. The only thing that kept him from being perfectly "movie-star gorgeous" was a small scar bisecting his left eyebrow. His hair was so dark it looked like black silk falling to his shoulders in soft waves that reflected the moon's light. "Devin, why would you ask for something that you know none of us are ever going to allow?"

"What harm will come from a conversation through the sealed door of a portal? Surely you do not believe my brother's powers are so great that he can pull the boy through the door?" Devin's voice was full of false bravado and when neither she nor Braden responded, he continued, "Kathleen, you are welcome to accompany us if you'd like. I would enjoy your company and I'm sure Damian would be quite pleased as well." The growling from her mates caused Devin to chuckle.

"I can see that idea is not something your mates approve of, but I'm fairly certain you are capable of making your own decisions when it comes to all things magical. Now, even you must be able to see that there is no reason for Braden to fear Damian since he is, after all, back behind the sealed portal doors by your own hand." Devin's eyes met hers, but Kit saw the diminished intensity so clearly it was distracting. Why would he continue to ask so meekly for something when she'd expected fire and passion-fueled demands?

"What is his interest in Braden?" Kit wasn't sure why she asked the question when she was certain it was all about power and control. But the minute she'd put the question out there she could see the uncertainty in Devin's eyes, and for just an instant, she thought he might be considering telling her the truth. In her opinion, the man standing in front of her wasn't at all certain what was going on either, and if Kit was going to make an informed guess, she'd bet he wasn't at all happy with the situation.

"You know precisely what his interest in Braden is about, Kathleen. Your attempt at naïveté is tiresome." Kit watched him and couldn't help tilting her head as she studied him. Speaking to the entire pack, she used their mind link to see if she was the only one seeing an incongruence. *'Am I the only one who thinks his words and his eyes are saying different things?'* After hearing the agreement of the others she added, *'It's time to end this conversation and do a little research. But I'm not sure he is going to let us walk away just yet.'*

"Devin, I don't know what's going on but I'm going to be asking some questions about the connection you are denying. I suggest you do the same. Braden is not going with you, now or in the future. Take that message back to your brother. Assure him that any attempts take Braden forcibly from our legal care will be met with considerable force."

Devin's eyes widened. "Legal care? Explain what that means. I am under the impression he has no living relatives."

Kit merely nodded. "Members of our pack have been granted permanent guardianship of Braden at his next of kin's request." She watched his eyes dart quickly giving her the impression that something had just clicked into place for him. *Spell me, I wish I knew what just went through his mind. I have the distinct impression that he's just figured out something vital and I don't like being on the outside of the knowledge circle.* Kit hadn't meant to broadcast that thought to her pack mates, but she obviously had, judging by their murmured agreements.

Devin's face seemed impassive for several seconds and then the blink her grandmother had told her to watch for broadcast his intention to move a split second before his arm received the message. Kit didn't see Braden move...hell, she doubted he had bothered. But the protective bubble that surrounded them all had materialized so quickly she'd heard gasps of surprise from every direction.

Kit had to smile to herself, Braden's move had been just as effective and not nearly as messy as hers had been last year with Damian. *Yeah, blowing beings back to their molecular base tends to be viewed as overkill by most people.*

143

When she refocused her attention on the wizard standing on the other side of the iridescent shield, she noted the sly smile moving over Devin's face. It was a look that said he knew something she didn't and that feeling made her more than just a bit uncomfortable. And then in flashy show of smoke and light, he was gone.

CHAPTER TWENTY

T HE NEXT AFTERNOON Kit sat in Jameson and Trevlon's office and watched her granny and mother execute one of the most amazing spells she'd ever seen. They had gathered the entire security team and numerous other interested parties, including Cecil, Marcus, and Reagan. Kit had questioned Marcus's presence and her granny had just patted her hand and promised that all things would be revealed to her when the time was right. Not a very comforting answer, in Kit's opinion, but about par for the course considering she been getting evasive answers like this one for her entire life.

But she tried to set all of that frustration aside as she watched in fascination as her mother and grandmother each took one of Braden's hands. After murmuring to him softly about how to open his mind to them, a shimmering mass appeared in the center of the room. For a few seconds it was merely a mass of swirling light and color, but slowly a finely detailed hologram of their encounter with Devin became visible in the center of the room and replayed in vivid three-dimensional detail. The fact they'd been able to use his memory to recreate the encounter was just wickedly amazing.

Since she had been the one speaking to Devin, Cecil had suggested using Braden's memory instead of her own, because he'd felt Kit's memory was likely much more one-dimensional, and Kit had appreciated the reprieve. Her grandmother and mother had both readily agreed and as they'd pulled Braden into the center of the room, the elderly wizard had looked over at her and winked. She'd known in that moment that he'd sensed how uncomfortable she'd been thinking about her mother getting that close. In truth, when they'd explained what they planned to do, it had seemed much too close to mindreading for Kit's comfort. The further Kit could keep her mother from her unspoken thoughts and emotions, the more peaceful things would be for everyone.

Tristan had spent a lot of time and effort setting up the video equipment so they'd be able to watch the session again and again, but Kit strongly doubted any of it would actually end up on tape since her mother had likely jammed the feeds before he'd even finished plugging in the last piece of sensitive electronic equipment. Carla Harris's paranoia about being photographed was well documented and a little thing like Cecil's warning wouldn't be enough to back her off.

Watching the scene through Braden's eyes only reinforced Kit's impression that Devin wasn't entirely committed to the task he'd been assigned. His hesitance was almost palatable. And when Kit asked him why his brother wanted Braden, it was obvious Devin was wondering the same thing. The second time they played it, Kit shifted her focus and watched her granny very closely. If she hadn't been paying very close attention, she most certainly would have missed the slight grimace at that point.

Jameson, could you please suggest a short break for refreshments? I'd like to ask Granny Good Witch a couple of questions in private. I'm particularly interested in having Braden out of the room.' While it was true that Kit had found the mind link communication horribly intrusive and annoying at first, she was discovering it was quite convenient on occasions like these. And in this instance she was eternally grateful to the Fates for providing it.

'Sure, kitten. Do you want one of us to stay? I know you are safe, but I don't really like having you out of reach.' Kit noted the affection in his voice and she turned to him and smiled.

'Thank you, but no. I'll be fine. I have a feeling that she knows more about the connection between Damian and Braden than she is telling.' And if history was anything to go by, Kit's observation was probably just the tip of the iceberg. Jameson quickly began clearing the room and just as Kit turned to speak with her grandmother, she noticed Marcus standing to the side leaning against the stone mantle over the fireplace. His pose was no doubt well-choreographed to look casual, but it was anything but. He looked every inch the Dominant Kit knew him to be. His salt and pepper hair was perfectly cut and layered back away from his high cheekbones and onyx colored eyes. His black slacks and shirt perfectly tailored to highlight his broad shoulders and narrow waist. His Italian leather shoes were black as well and broadcast his exquisite taste in fashion was equaled only in his desire for comfort. When he saw Kit looking at him, he merely raised a brow in question.

"Marcus, if you don't mind I would like to speak to my grandmother alone for a moment." Kit hadn't meant for her voice to sound quite so sharp, but she really didn't feel like dealing with him right now.

"Actually, Kathleen, I do mind. And I think you will find my input rather helpful." His voice had that hot and cold tone Doms used so effectively, and Kit had to press her lips together to keep from spouting the snarky retort that had nearly slipped free. He must have noticed her frustration because he smiled and walked toward her with all the elegance and grace of a jungle cat stalking its prey. "You know, sweet subbie, I can read your expressions perfectly and if you belonged to me, you'd already be stripped and over my knee."

Before Kit could even respond, her grandmother snorted from beside her. "Very dramatic, Marcus, but Kit doesn't belong to you—so can it." Kit tried to hold back her smile, but knew she'd failed miserably when Marcus just looked at her and shook his head.

Turning to her grandmother, Kit didn't waste any time because she knew they wouldn't be able to keep the others out for long. "What is the connection between Damian and Braden? And don't try to blow smoke up my ass, Granny, because I know there is one and I am convinced you know exactly what it is."

She saw Marcus go completely still beside her, and for a moment she wondered if he was rethinking his decision to stay. *Good. Maybe he's planning a hasty retreat.* Kit knew exactly how to play the advantage of knowing her grandmother so well. Ruby Stone was a skilled witch with the ability to shroud the truth in a thousand different cloaks, but she was not a liar. Kit had purposely phrased her question in a way that had left her granny with very little wiggle room. Ruby Stone was going to have to either lie or spill the truth. Kit watched as her grandmother fought whatever internal battle she was waging and Kit saw her eyes flit to Marcus more than once.

"Spell me, you could help out here, Marcus. After all, you have more at stake here than I do." Ruby was obviously frustrated and Marcus's soft chuckle didn't seem to improve her mood any.

"She didn't ask *me* anything, Ruby." Kit rolled her eyes at Marcus's reply and then cringed when he straightened and all but growled at her. "Kathleen, I'm going to take your disrespect up with your Masters."

"With all *due respect*, Master Marcus. We are not in your club, we are not *playing*, and I am not being disrespectful. You, on the other hand, are being quite rude to both my grandmother and me in my own home. You insinuated yourself into a private conversation and now you want to play semantics games. Quite frankly, I believe you are the one who is being disrespectful." Okay, Kit would concede that she was probably pushing the limits now, but damn he was an arrogant bastard at times, and she was really tired of him treating her like she was a dim wit. And his obvious, yet still unexplained, history with her grandmother was still a sore subject as well.

Glancing over at him, she had to hold back her laughter at his stunned expression. Obviously he wasn't accustomed to anyone speaking to him so bluntly. Right now she was operating on a limited timeline and she needed answers. Her grandmother heard people stirring in the hall and Kit rolled her wrist in the direction of the door until she heard the lock engage. "Stop stalling, I'm getting impatient and I can promise you Jameson and Trev will not appreciate being locked out of their own office because you decided to play this dance of deception game."

Ruby moved over to the windows and looked out over the enormous back meadow. "We have reason to believe that Braden may be a descendant of Damian's. We aren't sure, but there are a couple of ways to find out." Kit heard Marcus clear his throat behind her.

Turning to face him and knew her entire body was broadcasting her frustration, she said, "Marcus? Do you have something to contribute or are you simply editorializing? Because I have to tell you I'm finding your behavior uncharacteristically obnoxious."

"That's two, Kathleen." He took a deep breath and nodded to her grandmother. "I'll take this now, Ruby. I see no reason for us to continue hiding the facts. Braden is old enough to learn his heritage. Knowledge is power, he will be better prepared to make the right choices when the time comes if he has all the facts." He blew out a breath and for the first time since she'd met him, Kit noticed a thread of unease in the demeanor of one of the most influential Doms in New York.

Jameson and Trev had told Kit how well respected Marcus was when they had first introduced her to their friend and mentor. And then Kit had done a bit of research of her own as well. It seemed he was indeed incredibly well known in the lifestyle, but what had been interesting to Kit was the fact his club seemed to be little more than a very lucrative hobby. And even though it apparently was wildly successful, it certainly hadn't explained his vast wealth.

Marcus Hines' finances hadn't been easy to trace, but she'd found the puzzle interesting enough to follow the trail back several decades. In the end, she hadn't been able to find a beginning so she'd finally been forced to assume he'd merely inherited well. But now that she knew he was somehow connected to her granny, the chances were awfully good that he's had a *lot* of years to accumulate money. Over the years, Kit had observed that most people in the magical community had vast financial resources because they'd had so much longer to put things together. Most of them didn't use their magic in business...at least not directly, because it was considered unethical.

"Kitten?" Jameson's voice startled her and she blinked

up at him wondering how he'd managed to position himself right in front of her without her knowing it. *Damn it, I thought I locked the door. Now I'm never going to get Marcus to cough up the details.* Cursing her inattention, she smiled up at her Alpha. "Are you alright? You didn't even hear me come in." She knew what was coming next, hell, she could practically repeat the speech verbatim she'd heard it so often.

The "You Must Be Aware of Your Environment at All Times" speech was an oldie, but goodie. Unfortunately, Kit often found herself lost in thought and then she was on the receiving end of "the speech." Both Jameson and Trevlon had frequently wondered how she'd managed to avoid becoming a crime victim when she'd lived alone in the city. And it was probably a legitimate question because she was fairly sure being *disconnected* was not a new situation for her. *And how did he open that damned door?* Marcus was going to clam up for sure. *Damn and double damn. I was so close, too. Boy, I'm really hungry. Did I eat already?* She heard laughter and realized Braden was standing beside her.

"Holy cats, Kit. You were totally out there. Talk about your mental field trip. Probably should have had a passport for that one." Kit tried to be annoyed with his cheekiness, but he was finally feeling confident enough to let his real personality shine through and she just didn't have it in her to criticize him.

"Har-Har. Just what I need, another critic. Thanks for your support. You're a real pal, Braden." She chuckled when Braden grinned and blushed, they had developed an easy rapport, and Kit was continually amazed at the young man's easy going nature. Here was a kid who had lost both his parents, was a target of the dark side of magic, and had been seriously injured in the last abduction attempt, yet he still had an innocence that was completely endearing.

CHAPTER TWENTY-ONE

JAMESON STEPPED INTO their suite and blew out a sigh. He had known Kit was going to be off-the-chart steamed when he'd sent her upstairs to rest. He had reluctantly left her in their office to speak with her granny and then gone to Tristan's office to monitor what happened. Watching Marcus treat her like a wayward slave had made him see red. He'd seen Kit use magic to lock the doors and had chuckled. Did she really think he and Trev didn't have the doors set to automatically open as they approached? It really was a sweet bit of technology and they had been quite happy to have it installed on several of the doors around the estate.

When Kit hadn't noticed him enter, he'd spared a glance at Marcus who had merely shrugged further fueling his frustration with his longtime friend. But when he'd made his way over to his mate and she'd still been so lost in her thoughts she hadn't heard him, he'd actually become alarmed. He wasn't going to stand by and let her push herself to the point of complete exhaustion, and that was the edge she seemed to be skating on.

He'd stepped back with Angie and still regretted how far that situation had gone south before he'd called her in. Jameson didn't use his Alpha influence often and it was even rarer for he and Trev to tag team a pack member. And neither he nor his brother had enjoyed their little "sit down" with one of their favorite cousins. But once she'd calmed down enough to really listen to them, she'd agreed that the power struggle she was engaged in wasn't in anyone's best interest. Pulling the "you're hurting your mates, your patients, and *yourself*" card had been an act of desperation, but it had worked perfectly. Just the mention of hurting others brought the sweet submissive in Angie into play, no matter how much she hated it.

Jameson really had been pleased with the way their meeting had ended. Jameson had presented Angie with an offer of a position with the pack with a state of the art research lab built to her specifications thrown in to sweeten the deal. The catch had been that she only work a three quarters schedule and ironically, that had been a major sticking point for her. But Angie had finally agreed to scale back her schedule and prepare a compromise for her Alphas to consider. Sighing to himself, he was sure the coming confrontation with his mate wasn't going to go nearly as smoothly.

When he finally looked around the room, Jameson noticed his brother leaning against the edge of the large window in the living room. He had a drink in his hand and nodded his head to the bar where another sat. "Better fortify yourself. Our sweet mate is madder than a wet hen as our dad used to say."

"Where is she?" Jameson made his way to the bar and downed the scotch in two gulps, enjoying the burn as it spread out over his chest. "Are the twins here?" He didn't want them exposed to the fight he knew was coming. Anytime Ryan sensed any distress in his mama things started moving around the room. And the more unhappy Kit was, the more things tended to topple to the floor and shatter. Adana, on the other hand, simply watched with detached interest unless he or Trev became agitated. Their little princess loved her daddies and anyone on the receiving end of their anger got a healthy second dose of pissy-pintsized witch for dessert.

The last time her grandma Carla had thrown barbs at him, Adana had managed to turn her grandmother's hair a nice shade of moss green. Jameson was sure it was because Trev had been envisioning their caustic mother-in-law as a toad sitting in the lily pads out back, but he couldn't prove it. "Letting your mind wander like that isn't a very good way to show Kit how important is to stay focused." His brother's laughter had Jameson shaking his head. Hell, his brother was right. Here he was poised to confront their mate about how dangerous her distraction and fatigue was, and he wasn't any better.

"There isn't anything about this that is going to win me any points in the short run. Long term…well, I think she'll see that we are right, but she isn't going to be happy at first. And when she finds out her granny put a spell on the suite to restrict her magic for tonight, she is going to blow a gasket for sure." The spell had actually been Ruby's idea and he'd readily agreed that this one needed to be played out with their roles more traditionally defined. Kit didn't use magic often in her everyday life, but when she became emotional random things tended to happen.

Turning toward the hallway, he asked, "Is she in the shower? I thought I heard it when I came in."

Trev nodded, "Yes, and she's obviously hiding." Setting the crystal tumbler he'd drained on top of the bar, he moved toward Jameson. "Come on, the sooner we get this over with…the sooner we can get to the make-up sex." Their chuckles both sounded hallow and a tread of dreaded concern moved through Jameson's mind. What if she left them? He'd never survive the heartache. Most male shifters didn't survive long after losing a mate, particularly when the mate chose to leave.

Stepping in to the master suite's enormous bath, the first thing Jameson noticed was that the steam was so thick he could barely see across the room. And then he picked up the faint sound of a sniffle, and his heart shattered. Stepping around the glass block wall and into the shower, he saw Kit crumbled on the floor facing away from him and her shaking shoulders let him know that she was sobbing but holding in as much of the sound as possible. Grateful that he'd already shed everything but his well-worn jeans on the way through their bedroom, he stepped into the shower and picked her up. He hated feeling her stiffen in his arms but hearing her whispered, "No, I don't want you," shredded the few pieces of his heart that hadn't fallen into his stomach when he'd first heard her crying.

When she tried to pull away from him and scramble out of his hold, he tightened his arms around her. "Kitten. Stop." He rarely used his compelling voice, but he'd certainly used it this time because her safety was at stake. Her skin was so slick from the water that he was worried about dropping her and nothing good was going to come from her falling out of his arms. She'd immediately stilled even though he could feel her mind pressing against his. Trev was holding one of the warm towels from the heated bar and tucked in around her.

"Trev, please take me. I don't want to talk to Jameson." Kit's voice was starting to regain some of the heat he'd been expecting. He had been prepared to deal with a pissed off mate, not the defeated one he'd found on the shower floor.

"No can do, baby. This is about all three of us working

this out. We love you more than life itself, but we won't let you play us against each other. It isn't in anyone's best interest for us to do that." Jameson gave his brother a quick nod letting him know he appreciated his comments. He sat on the small sofa facing the fireplace and settled her on his lap. He unpinned her hair and let the beautiful waterfall of dark red curls fall down her back. Kit still hadn't met his gaze, instead she was staring into the flickering gas flames.

"Kitten, I know you are upset with me, so why don't you tell me what the problem is and let's see if we can't work through it." She didn't respond for so long that he'd started to wonder if he wasn't going to have to compel her cooperation. He had a very real aversion to using that technique and Trev had always steadfastly refused to ever employ his compelling voice. But Jameson didn't plan to let this problem fester between them either. She could either answer on her own or he'd force the issue.

"You swore you would never hurt me...and you did." He felt her body shiver and he wasn't sure if it was from the conversation or if she was really cold. Jameson silently asked Trev to retrieve her robe. Once they'd gotten her covered he'd pulled her back onto his lap.

"Now, please explain what I did that hurt you, kitten. Because I don't want to make any assumptions here. You are much too precious to both of us for us to risk misinter-preting."

She finally turned to him and blew out a shaky breath. Sitting with her long, slender fingers fisted in her lap, she shot him a look that made him grateful her magic wasn't available at this moment. "You sent me out of the room like an errant child. You basically told everyone in the house that you don't value my input, that the questions I wanted my grandmother to answer were of no consequence, and that you didn't want me to be seen as a management problem to Marcus...who, by the way, was an arrogant ass." This time when she tried to stand up he let her—mostly because she was so surprised by her words. He barely managed to pull back his gut reaction, which was to roar out his disagreement with her assessment. This time he decided to try to see the incident from her viewpoint, but he was coming up empty.

He and Trev spoke quietly via their mind link and by mutual agreement, they agreed to give her a moment and they just watched as she paced in front of the living room's large array of windows. They'd seen her do this several time when something that was bothering her. True to form, she paced quickly back and forth in front of the large windows muttering her frustration as if no one else was in the room. He wasn't catching it all but he had heard enough to know that she was royally pissed at Marcus and was questioning his mother's marital status when she'd had the "piss ant with the ego the size of the Great Pyramids." He knew she was mentally processing what had happened and he didn't mind waiting for her to see she was overreacting.

She came to a sudden stop and turned slowly to stare at him. Her hands were fisted on her slender hips and her eyes narrowed. "Overreacting? Are you fucking kidding me, Jameson?" Usually Kit's strong emotions caused the candles in the room to suddenly burst into flames so they kept the room well stocked so she didn't burn the mansion down. But this time every candle in the room melted in to a puddle before seemingly evaporating into thin air.

Holy fucking meltdown. Did you see that? I thought her granny did a little hocus pocus to keep Kit's magic in check tonight?

"And you think I didn't pick up Granny Good Witch's trace magic the minute I stepped into the suite? Really? Spell me, you two are un-fucking-believable. Did you think I'd use magic on you?" Her voice was going up with every word she spoke and Jameson was getting worried that she was going to fly right apart considering how she was literally vibrating with rage. It was definitely time to regain control of this discussion.

"Kathleen, sit down and listen. *Now!*" She might have been righteously pissed, but he was still her Alpha and she sat down despite the fact she'd fixed him with her best *eat shit and die* expression.

"First of all, the spell wasn't our idea so put that notion right out of your pretty little head. Second, you were sent up here to rest because I not only entered the room, but walked right up in front of you without you even realizing I was close. It is painfully obvious to everyone but you that you are physically and emotionally exhausted. I made poor decisions with Angie recently and I was determined to not repeat it with you." Scrubbing his hand over his face in frustration, he stood and walked to the fireplace and leaned against the black onyx mantle. Almost immediately he felt a lot of his frustration drain away and the infusion of energy that followed was a welcome relief.

While he gathered his thoughts, Trev leaned forward with his elbows resting on his knees and clasped his hands. "Kit, we watched from Tristan's office." When she gasped and started to stand he held out his hand. "Hear us out. We weren't spying on you, we were watching over you. We are your mates, baby, and your safety is our chief concern. And to be perfectly honest, we know Marcus can be a real ass hat sometimes and we were neither one particularly pleased that he'd stayed behind. We weren't sure what his interest was, but as it turns out, we were right to be concerned."

Jameson watched as Kit mulled over Trev's words. He could almost hear the well-oiled wheels of her mind spinning rapidly as she tried to make sense of everything that Trev had said. The dark circles under her eyes told him just how little sleep she'd gotten last night after their run. She still hadn't regained the weight she'd lost recently, and that only added to her fragile appearance and emotional vulnerability. "Kitten, we happen to agree with you that Marcus was out of line. His request that we take you in hand because you were disrespectful was out of line at the minimum and probably closer to completely inappropriate. Honestly, I've never known Marcus's ego to be such a problem, but where you and your granny are concerned he just can't seem to behave himself."

Shaking his head, he remembered how outraged Marcus had been when they'd told him clearly that he'd been out of line and that they agreed with Kit. They had actually been quite proud of the way she'd handled the situation, but he wasn't sure she was ready to hear that just yet. Drawing a deep breath, he decided to just spit out the worst of the information they'd gotten after she'd left the room and then work from there. "Kit, Marcus's interest in all this is pretty significant. And Devin wasn't delusional when he referred to Reagan as his sister-in-law."

Her eyes had gone wide and he could see her gripping her knees so hard her knuckles had gone white. "What do you mean?"

"Damian and Marcus are brothers. Marcus is the light to Damian's dark, although after his behavior tonight I'm not sure *light* is quite the word I would have chosen." Jameson had just gotten the last word out when everything seemed to happen in slow motion around him. Kit sprang to her feet and she'd gone completely ashen as all the blood seemed to have drained from her face. Her eyes went wide and then rolled up so far all he could see was white. Before he could even take a step forward she was falling. Her knees had simply folded out from under her. Trev caught her just as her forehead hit the marble end table with a deafening thud.

Chapter Twenty-Two

TREVLON WOLF COULDN'T remember a time when he'd felt more helpless. Even though he'd moved the instant he saw the blood drain from Kit's beautiful face, he had still failed to prevent her from being injured. Cursing the repeat of his earlier failure, he stood by and tried to tamp down the urge to drive his fist through the nearest wall. For now all he could do was stand by and watch as Angie assessed the damage and try to focus on anything but drowning in the feelings of guilt that were crashing over him. *God damn it to hell. This is the second time I've failed to protect her. How can she ever trust me again?* Trev hadn't intentionally broadcast his thoughts to his brother, but he hadn't tried to hide them either so it wasn't a surprise when Jameson leveled him with a look before responding.

'We are both responsible…equally culpable. I knew the news was going to shock her. I should have been closer as well. How we continually manage to fuck up with the most important person in the world I can't imagine. It is times like these that I miss our dads the most.' Jameson's feelings of loneliness bled over to Trev and he felt as swamped by the emotion as his brother.

Angie huffed out an exasperated breath and turned to them. "Would you two overbearing whiny asses mind taking it outside so you can speak aloud and stop bothering your mate? Your incessant chatter may not be out loud, but it's still a pain in the ass." Jameson blinked at her in surprise and Angie just shook her head as if she couldn't imagine how he could possibly be so dim. "No, I can't hear you...I'm just getting static, but I know Kit can by the changes in her heart rate." Waving toward the door, she added, "I'll be out in a minute to speak with you. And find Ruby, please." Jameson was actually somewhat stunned when his cousin turned her back on him as if he'd been dismissed. Blinking back his surprise, he stalked from the room.

ANGIE WANTED TO giggle at the look on Jameson's face. He'd obviously become comfortable in his role as the Wolf Pack's Alpha and wasn't accustomed to being sent from the room. When Kit's cold fingers clenched her hand Angie's attention snapped back to her patient's ashen colored face in time to see her mouth "Thanks."

"My pleasure. Boy, sometimes men just don't get it. I assume they were playing the World Cup of the Blame game?" Kit didn't open her eyes, but her smile said it all. When Angie had arrived the first thing she'd done was make sure all the lights were dimmed because the huge lump on the back of Kit's face told her that the woman was going to likely wake up with a blinding headache and light was going to be excruciating. When Angie had checked her pupils Kit had groaned and tried to turn away from the light. "Sorry for that, sweet sister, but I need to make sure you are alright. That is a nasty bump you've got on the back of your head." Angie had made sure she'd spoken softly and watched closely as Kit relax back into her pillow. "Your granny should be able to help since I don't think you have any real neurological problems. I'll send her in after I fill her in. We'll talk out in the hall because I know your head must be pounding like a bitch." Kit's smile let Angie know she'd been right.

KIT LEANED BACK against the cool cotton pillowcase and knew immediately it was Trev's. From the beginning she'd been able to tell the men apart not only by scent, but their energies were vastly different as well. She wondered briefly if her life would ever be simple again. Before she'd mated, she hadn't struggled with any of the problems she was facing now and it was often just as overwhelming as she'd feared it would be. She had avoided large gatherings of witches or shifters for years because she'd feared finding her mate. And then she walked into a mid-town dance club and was slammed full force into the very situation she'd sworn she'd never let herself get caught up in.

She was grateful that Angie had dimmed the lights and was keeping everyone out of the room for a bit to give her a chance to rest. Obviously she'd spoken to Jameson and Trev about their mind link communication as well, because everything had been blissfully quiet for over an hour. The fact that Marcus was Damian's brother was almost too much to take in. She remembered Jameson saying something about him being *light* to Damian's *dark*, but she wasn't entirely convinced Marcus was exactly pure as the driven snow.

It was obvious that her granny wasn't overly fond of the man, and that alone was cause for concern. She'd never known her grandmother to misjudge anyone, so Kit wasn't planning to let her guard down anytime soon. Reagan had mentioned something about *his story to tell* so evidently she knew at least part of Marcus's story. She was sure her mates would have mentioned Damian to Marcus. They'd no doubt shared what had happened with Damian right after she'd first met the Wolf brothers, so why hadn't he told them then that the demon threatening her was his brother? Or had he and they'd failed to tell her?

Thinking that they'd withheld a secret that earth shattering from her was inconceivable. *'It had damned well be, kitten.'* Jameson's voice slid through her mind like a warm touch and she couldn't help but feel comforted knowing he'd been listening silently. He and Trev had told her in the beginning that she'd eventually come to rely on the connection and find strength in knowing they were only a thought away. She'd doubted them, but in a flash of insight, she understood exactly what they'd been meant.

She thought she'd heard the door but when she blinked open her eyes, she looked up into the kind eyes of her grandfather. "Gramps? How?" Losing her grandfather had been one of the most difficult times in Kit's life. They'd been so close and she still felt his absence each and every day. He smiled at her and just studied her as he'd done so often as she'd been growing up.

"The love that surrounds you shines through your eyes, princess." Kit had so many questions…so many things she wanted to tell him, but she was afraid to speak again for fear her delusion might be scattered back into her mind if she did anything more than breathe. "You can talk to me, it's alright. I promise to stay for a bit. Your granny knows I'm here so she'll keep the others at bay for a little while." The fact that he still spoke to his wife was oddly comforting even as it was hard to wrap her mind around. "We do talk…often, but it isn't the same as being able to hold each other. Don't ever underestimate the power of touch, princess."

For just a moment, Kit was overcome with the enormity of her emotions. The sweet feeling of familiarity was so powerful she was glad she was already lying down. "I've missed you so much. You just can't possibly know how much. So often I've held Ryan and Adana wishing I could introduce you to them." She felt the tears rolling down her cheeks but didn't even try to hold them back.

"Those were the moments I was standing right beside you, princess. I'm never far from you. I am so proud of you. You're growing in to the amazing wife and mother I always knew you'd be." He seemed to be lost in thought for several seconds before his focus returned to her. Again she was wrapped in the comfort of something familiar, because watching him focusing on his thoughts in the midst of a conversation was something he'd done so often when he'd still be on this side of death's veil.

"Can you tell me what it's like…what it's like on the other side?"

He smiled at her and she saw the dimples she'd always loved so much. "I could, but you wouldn't believe me." She heard his chuckle and her heart clenched when she realized how much she'd missed hearing his laughter. "Princess, I don't want you to be sad, that isn't why I'm here." Kit nodded and tried to pull back the flood of tears that was so close to falling. "I'm here to help prepare you because the battles you'll face in the future will require everything in you. They aren't immediate, but you've got so very much to learn and it's coming sooner than you think. You are right about Marcus. He isn't perfect, and believe me when I tell you that I know because we were friends for many, many years. But then…princess, no one is *all* good just as no one is *all* bad. There are shades of gray in each and every person you meet. Your job is to recognize both the yin and yang, and learn how to channel the power of both sides to your benefit." Kit considered his words and couldn't hold back her grin because it was so typical of the advice he'd given her so often as she was growing up.

"But, Gramps, it's often so very difficult to distinguish between those who are helping paddle your canoe and those who are drilling holes in it. The stakes are getting so high that I'm terrified of making a mistake." Kit didn't want to even hazard a guess about how dire the consequences could be if she mistook an enemy for a friend. Just thinking about Marcus Hines' connection to Damian sent a shiver of fear up her spine.

"I know the news about Marcus has unsettled you, but if you shut him out you'll be denying yourself a very powerful alley. Marcus can be an arrogant ass, but his magic is just as powerful as his brother's." She saw him grin and recognized the look as one that reminded her of all the fun times they'd had sharing mischief. "I was quite proud of the way you stood up to him a bit ago you know. He might have been angry, but your men set him straight and in the end he'll respect you a lot more now."

When she'd first seen him sitting beside her, he'd appeared almost solid but he was starting to fade. His expression softened as he spoke, "I'm getting tired, princess. Holding this form requires a lot of energy and I want to say a couple of more things before we have to part once again. First, your mates are among the most honorable men you could have ever found and they love you to the depths of their souls. Be grateful for the blessings you've been given."

"You said the battle is coming...how will I know? Will you be near me then?" She could hear the panic in her voice and tears were already starting to fill her eyes.

"I'm always near. Your children can still see me because their hearts are so pure." His voice lowered as if he were whispering, "They don't like your mother much, and I've helped them play with her a bit. I'm hoping she gets smart before their magic really gives her trouble." His chuckle was faint and he was becoming much less distinct. "You'll know because you will feel the urgency surround you…I know that is vague, but I'm not allowed to alter your fate, just guide you."

"Please don't go…I have so many questions. I miss you so much." Kit had given up trying to hold back the tears and felt them flowing freely down her cheeks. He'd already faded until he was just a shadow floating toward the ceiling and Kit already felt empty in his absence. She could hear voices right outside her door and knew she wouldn't be alone much longer.

Suddenly realizing that the horrible pain of the headache she'd been battling was gone, she felt warmth move through her and whispered her thanks for his healing help. Kit couldn't remember a time when she'd been given a better reminder of the power of the Universe. *Because it surrounds me each and every day I often forget how much magic there is, and how blessed I've been. I'll miss you each and every day, Gramps. Send me signs that I'm on the right path if you can.*

Suddenly she was surrounded by a warmth that was more than just the air around her. It was a feeling of love and acceptance that reached all the way to her soul and his voice floated through her mind, "Watch for the feathers, princess…" The door had opened and just as they wrapped her safely in their arms, Kit looked up to see a iridescent blue feather wafting back and forth slowly making its way down until it landed with a shimmer of light right in front of his picture on her dresser.

EPILOGUE

K IT LEANED BACK against Trev's chest and looked out over the festivities in their backyard. Braden's grandmother had been visiting for the past two weeks and she was leaving in the morning. Her position at the university required her to be back before the beginning of the fall term and it was going to be difficult to see the spritely older woman leave. The pack had combined her going away party with their annual last big bash of the summer, and every pack member had turned out to celebrate their new friend and the coming fall. Jameson leaned over from his chaise lounge and grasped her hand. "Are you alright, kitten? You seemed to be a million miles away."

There wasn't any use denying her distraction. The previous weeks had been a flurry of training and revelations. Watching Braden mature right before her eyes had given her a new appreciation for how quickly her own babies were going to grow up and Kit had been spending a lot of time playing with both Ryan and Adana. Even at their ages, their magical abilities were already easy to see. And when Kit noticed either of them seeming to focus on something over her shoulder she always whispered a greeting to her grandfather.

"No, I'm fine. There has just been a lot to process recently. Meeting Braden has been a blessing in so many ways and I know he hates to see his grandmother leave, but he knows he needs to process all she'd told him as well." Kit knew her words were an enormous understatement. And she found herself wondering how a child dealt with everything that had been thrown at him and maintain the positive attitude and sweet spirit Braden exhibited each day.

Feeling Trev's arms tighten around her, she let him siphon off some of the strain from her muscles as only he could. "Baby, no man—no matter his age—wants to find out his mother was the product of a forced encounter with a black-hearted demon." Kit agreed, but she'd been impressed with how thoughtful and kind Dr. O'Donnell had been with her explanation. She'd assured Braden that even though her time with Damian had been among the darkest and most frightening experiences of her life, she wouldn't have traded any of the years she spent in fear of him finding out her daughter belonged to him or the heartache of losing her only child. She'd told her grandson that all of the tears had been worth it because they'd given her a daughter that she had loved more than life itself, and she'd gotten a grandson who was making her very proud as well.

"She really did a great job of helping him accept his heritage. And I'm glad he has chosen to honor both his mother's and his father's memories by staying true to the Light." 'Because the Dark Side can sure paint a tempting picture.'

Jameson leaned forward and kissed the tip of her nose. 'Indeed that is true, but it isn't just true for witches and wizards, kitten.'

Kit sighed at the truth of his words and just spent several long moments watching the festivities around them. She let her mind wander until Trev finally squeezed her in his arms. "What are you thinking about that has your mind whirling light a wind turbine in a hurricane, baby?"

"I was wondering what's headed our way next." The truth was that Kit was more than a little worried about what the Fates had in store for them. Her grandfather's warning had not fallen on deaf ears. And Kit and Braden had both stepped up their training so they'd be ready. "Braden is so very talented and has so many hopes and dreams. Well...it seems a shame for him to be kept a virtual prisoner in the confines of the estate for an indefinite period of time."

Jameson leaned forward and grasped her hand. "Kitten, Cecil mentioned taking Braden to visit the Supreme Council. There is a chance that he'd get to mentor with one of the Council members. It seems that your granny has done about all she can with both of you." She was looking into his eyes and knew there was something else...something he hadn't yet said, but she just waited. They might not have been married for a long time, but they were *mates* so the connection between them was deeper. And right now everything in his expression spoke of hesitance and worry.

He took her hands in his much larger ones and rubbed circles in her palms with his thumbs. Trev had pulled her hair to the side and was pressing his lips against her pulse point and sending tingles up her spine despite her worry about what they *weren't saying*. Jameson finally took a deep breath and she knew he'd made the decision to tell her what was bothering him.

"Kitten, Cecil also asked us to let you go with them." When she gasped, he held up his hand to stop her from interrupting. "Let me finish. Please, because this is very difficult. Trev and I want you to know we won't make that decision for you. We would rather you didn't leave us and our children, but we won't stop you if that's where your heart's desire is."

Kit felt her eyes fill with tears as her heart swelled with love for her mates. As her Alphas and as her mates, they could have easily made the call and kept her home. But they hadn't. They were letting her make her own decision and she couldn't think of anything else they could have done that would have demonstrated their love and respect for her any more clearly. She pulled his hands up to her lips and kissed each knuckle while trying to regain her composure.

"The only thing that will ever get me to leave my home and my family is an emergency that involves the life of another. I won't leave to train with a mentor who could easily travel here." Kit's answer was interrupted by the tapping of heels across the cobblestones.

Julie Wolf-Edwards stepped into their view and grinned. "Sorry to interrupt the romantic moment you have going here, but I have some pretty amazing news. And quite frankly I didn't want to wait to share it...I'm pushy that way." Her grin belied her snarky tone and Kit couldn't help but smile. "It seems our sweet Braden is exactly where he needs to be. While I've been holed up in the city I had some time to research some of the things that weren't adding up." Julie noticed Jameson's raised brow and shrugged her shoulders. "Hey...I talk to people okay? I missed my family and I called pack members to find out what was happening. Well, anyway...I kept getting different versions of the same event and that didn't make any sense to me. So I started charting the common links in all the inconsistencies and amazingly none of it led to Kit."

"Well, thanks...I think." Kit laughed even though she

was fairly certain it hadn't been a compliment.

Julie just rolled her eyes and continued, "They common links were Braden and Angie. Did you know that according to Braden's paternal history he is linked to the same packs as Angie's ancestors? And did you know that his maternal ancestors have displayed a remarkable ability to pull energy from those they are genetically linked to?" In a sudden flash of insight, Kit understood exactly what Devin had figured out and it didn't bode well for Angie's safety.

Kit had no sooner made the connection than Jameson's phone beeped and Kit watched his face pale as she checked the message. "That was Tristan…Angie's missing."

The End

Books by Avery Gale

The Wolf Pack Series
Mated – Book One
Fated Magic – Book Two
Tempted by Darkness – Book Three

Masters of the Prairie Winds Club
Out of the Storm
Saving Grace
Jen's Journey
Bound Treasure
Punishing for Pleasure
Accidental Trifecta
Missionary Position

The ShadowDance Club
Katarina's Return – Book One
Jenna's Submission – Book Two
Rissa's Recovery – Book Three
Trace & Tori – Book Four
Reborn as Bree – Book Five
Red Clouds Dancing – Book Six
Perfect Picture – Book Seven

Club Isola

Capturing Callie – Book One

Healing Holly – Book Two

Claiming Abby – Book Three

I would love to hear from you!

Email:

avery.gale@ymail.com

Website:

www.averygalebooks.com/index.html

Facebook:

facebook.com/avery.gale.3

Instagram:

avery.gale

Twitter:

@avery_gale